Readers love *Can't Live Without You* by ANDREW GREY

"This story was so fresh and new—and so well written and planned out, it was a pleasure to read from beginning to end."
—Alpha Book Club

"*Can't Live Without You* was like the best comfort food. It was feeling like your dreams were lost only to realize they were simply in hibernation."
—Diverse Reader

"Sweet, wonderful characters who overcome their sad past and find a way to carve a future together."
—Hearts on Fire Book Reviews

CAN'T LIVE WITHOUT YOU

ANDREW GREY

"This is an amazing read that left me… speechless, sad, angry, and happy."
—Gay Book Reviews

More praise for
ANDREW GREY

Cleansing Flame

"For fans of the author—you'll love this—and for someone looking for a nice, sweet, hurt/comfort romance with a bonus, historical story—this is for you!"

—The Blogger Girls

"This was such a well-written story and the plot was woven together so perfectly, I couldn't have asked for more."

—Alpha Book Club

Poppy's Secret

"If you love a good second chance story, family, cute kids and an allover fabulous romance with a touch of hot man sex you will love this."

—TTC Books and More

"I really enjoyed reading this sweet story."

—Gay Book Reviews

Planting His Dream

"Andrew Grey gives us another good book about finding love and holding on to it despite tremendous odds."

—The Blogger Girls

"Yet again Andrew Grey has managed to capture my imagination by presenting a deceptively simple situation in a light that made it interesting, revealing, and very moving. Bravo!"

—Rainbow Book Reviews

"This was a very well written book from an author I've grown to love."

—Inked Rainbow Reads

By Andrew Grey (cont.)

HOLIDAY STORIES
Copping a Sweetest Day Feel
Cruise for Christmas
A Lion in Tails
Mariah the Christmas Moose
A Present in Swaddling Clothes
Simple Gifts
Snowbound in Nowhere • Stardust

LAS VEGAS ESCORTS
The Price • The Gift

LOVE MEANS…
Love Means… No Shame
Love Means… Courage
Love Means… No Boundaries
Love Means… Freedom
Love Means … No Fear
Love Means… Healing
Love Means… Family
Love Means… Renewal
Love Means… No Limits
Love Means… Patience
Love Means… Endurance

LOVE'S CHARTER
Setting the Hook • Ebb and Flow

PLANTING DREAMS
Planting His Dream
Growing His Dream

REKINDLED FLAME
Rekindled Flame • Cleansing Flame

SENSES
Love Comes Silently • Love Comes
in Darkness • Love Comes Home

Love Comes Around • Love Comes
Unheard • Love Comes to Light

SEVEN DAYS
Seven Days • Unconditional Love

STORIES FROM THE RANGE
A Shared Range
A Troubled Range
An Unsettled Range
A Foreign Range
An Isolated Range
A Volatile Range • A Chaotic Range

STRANDED
Stranded • Taken

TALES FROM KANSAS
Dumped in Oz • Stuck in Oz
Trapped in Oz

TASTE OF LOVE
A Taste of Love
A Serving of Love
A Helping of Love
A Slice of Love

WITHOUT BORDERS
A Heart Without Borders
A Spirit Without Borders

WORK OUT
Spot Me • Pump Me Up
Core Training • Crunch Time
Positive Resistance
Personal Training
Cardio Conditioning
Work Me Out
(Print Only Anthology)

Published by DREAMSPINNER PRESS
www.dreamspinnerpress.com

NEVER LET YOU GO

ANDREW GREY

Published by

DREAMSPINNER PRESS

5032 Capital Circle SW, Suite 2, PMB# 279, Tallahassee, FL 32305-7886 USA
www.dreamspinnerpress.com

This is a work of fiction. Names, characters, places, and incidents either are the product of
author imagination or are used fictitiously, and any resemblance to actual persons, living or
dead, business establishments, events, or locales is entirely coincidental.

Never Let You Go
© 2017 Andrew Grey.

Cover Art
© 2017 L.C. Chase.
http://www.lcchase.com
Cover content is for illustrative purposes only and any person depicted on the cover is a
model.

ISBN: 978-1-63533-950-5
Digital ISBN: 978-1-63533-951-2
Library of Congress Control Number: 2017948497
Published September 2017
v. 1.0

Printed in the United States of America
∞
This paper meets the requirements of
ANSI/NISO Z39.48-1992 (Permanence of Paper).

To Dominic, I will never let you go.
And to Geri and Heidi—this idea was born of the three of us.
Thank you.

PROLOGUE

One Year Ago

Ashton Williams parked under one of the apple-shaped streetlights on Main Street and got out of his old gray Taurus. He leaned back down to grab his hated cane and then closed the car door. Standing still, he turned to the right and left, looking up and down the street. It hadn't changed much at all. The place still had the same small-town feel it always had. Ash remembered bounding up the steps of the library when he was in high school so he could see if they had a copy of the latest movie or a video game he'd wanted. Books, not so much, but games and videos—he'd been all about those.

He took a step around the car, heading away from traffic and onto the sidewalk. The drugstore was just down the block, and damn it all, he wasn't so crippled that half a block was too far to walk. Maybe he should have waited until he'd had more therapy and the doctors decided if he should have surgery on his knee. Ash had been making progress and everyone said he needed to be patient. Ash stopped, pushing those memories from his mind. That wasn't why he was here, and those thoughts did nothing but bring him back to the brink of the gaping hole of despair he'd been thrown into for months. He needed to put that behind him, at least during the day. Nights were another matter, but during the day, he was determined to look forward to what he'd had and could have once again.

Ash's heart beat a little faster as he walked closer to the store where Brighton worked. He was so properly named; at least Ash had always thought so. One look from his stunning blue eyes could push away the heaviest clouds. Even recalling them in his

1

mind's eye allowed him to get through months of confinement in rooms and holes where he could barely move, stomach empty, throat parched, wishing he could die but knowing Brighton was out there, waiting for him. Ash had stored the sunshine in those eyes in his mind, holding them precious, letting those eyes framed by flowing blond curls carry him through hell and out the other side. The photograph he'd had was long gone. It had fallen apart months ago. Ash had worn it out, but he carried the image with him where no one could get to it.

He'd called the telephone number he had for Brighton three times, each with the same response that the number was no longer in service, and when he checked the internet, it pointed him to the number he already had. That only added to his need to get here and see if he could find Brighton in case something had happened to him.

He moved on, getting closer now. Ash knew Brighton's schedule at work, at least the one he'd been working before he'd left. Ash hadn't wanted to leave, but he'd had no choice, and saying goodbye to Brighton had been the hardest, most heartbreaking thing he'd ever had to do. It was supposed to be his last assignment, two weeks and then he'd be able to use up his remaining leave and he'd be done, free, out… and his life would be his own once again. And now it was, at least what was left of it. He'd been discharged, sure enough, but he was left a shell of a man, and not just his injured body. His insides were hollow, and Ash wasn't even sure who he was any longer. All he knew was that he needed to get back to Brighton, so as soon as he'd been released and his debriefings were completed, he'd taken off, against the doctor's wishes. Everything inside him pulled him to Brighton.

Now he was back in his hometown, where he and Brighton had first met in middle school, though it was years later that they'd reconnected and something had clicked between them. Ash still couldn't believe it had been at a church social his aunt—Petunia to everyone else, but Aunt Petey to him—and

2

only remaining family member had asked him to attend. He'd expected an evening of old ladies and helping Aunt Petey with whatever she needed.

Ash raised his eyes to the sky, letting the heat from the sun warm his face and dry the tears that threatened. He'd already been to see her in the nursing home and was determined to get her the hell out of there.

"One thing at a time," he whispered to himself. That was another symptom of his incarceration at the hands of the enemy: he talked to himself all the time. It was a way to feel less lonely and had become a habit. He needed to let go of it because it tended to freak other people out. He lifted his gaze as he continued his slow steps toward his goal.

The door to the drugstore opened and a man stepped out. Ash knew him instantly—the height, or lack of it, slight build, floppy curls. Brighton needed a haircut, but he was still the man Ash had thought of and dreamed about every single time he'd closed his eyes for the last nine months. His body ached all over, and Ash felt Brighton's pull as strongly as the gravity of the sun.

Ash took a few steps, for a few seconds forgetting the cane and his aching leg. They didn't matter. All that did was how close he was and removing the last bit of distance that had spanned months and thousands of miles. Brighton turned away without looking, heading farther from him. He wasn't walking fast, but Ash was even slower, regardless of how much he pushed. Somehow Ash managed to pick up his pace, needing to get closer. The man he carried in his heart so deep, who had gotten him through hell and allowed him to come back, was just ahead, so close he could see him.

Ash opened his mouth to call out as Brighton stopped at the door to the coffee shop, holding it open as someone emerged. Another man, someone Ash didn't recognize, fell into step with Brighton, heading to the corner. They waited for the light, and Ash moved forward while they stopped. He was so damn close.

3

ANDREW GREY

"Brighton," Ash called, but the sound went nowhere. His throat was so dry, the cry came out as a whisper. He wet his mouth and swallowed multiple times, unable to take his gaze away. Ash's heart raced, his blood pounding a staccato beat in his ears. This was it. He was close, and all he could think about was how he was going to get to taste Brighton's sweet lips and feel his smooth, hot skin under his hands, and have someone to hold and see him through the nights when the inevitable nightmares came.

Ash stopped walking as Brighton leaned into the other man's touch. It was then that Ash saw the other man's hand rested on the small of Brighton's back, protectively, lovingly, the way Ash had always done. The light changed, and they crossed the street together. Ash told himself that they could just be friends and got his feet moving once again. Brighton was within sight and so close.

But then Ash stopped dead in his tracks, unable to move, as the man walking with Brighton leaned closer, his face disappearing behind Brighton's head. Ash knew he'd kissed him. He couldn't move. Suddenly his feet were so heavy, he couldn't lift them. He leaned entirely on his cane, hoping it didn't buckle under his weight, because if it did, he was going down. Ash didn't give a fuck. The physical pain would be preferable to the ache that settled where his heart had been, growing more and more acute until each breath became a stabbing pain. He'd seen movies, plenty of them, and he always thought that expression actors used when their heart had broken was fake. Well, it wasn't. He knew, because when he turned, the mask of pain reflected in the plate glass window was that exact expression. Combined with it was a sharp tearing he knew was his heart shattering into a million little pieces before scattering to the breeze.

He lifted his gaze to where Brighton had been but didn't see him. They were gone, most likely into the diner across the street. Ash thought about going over himself, but he knew what he would find and couldn't take it. The thought of Brighton, the person he

4

loved, the man who'd sworn he'd wait for him, his soul mate and the reason Ash had survived that hellhole for months…. Ash couldn't even bring himself to say the words.

That same gaping maw of blackness that had dogged him through months of interrogation opened in front of him again. More than once he'd thought of throwing himself into it and bringing the pain to an end. But he hadn't. He'd been stronger than that, and he still was, dammit. Ash turned around and lifted his gaze to where his car was parked. He hadn't really gone that far, thank God. At least he could make it back and then, in the semiprivacy of his own vehicle, he could fall apart.

A few minutes later, Ash fumbled to open the car door and threw the cane inside, the metal rod banging against the far window before falling onto the floor of the back seat. He managed to get inside and close the door, then leaned forward, resting his head on the steering wheel.

In the few minutes he'd been gone, the car had turned into an oven, and when Ash closed his eyes, he was right back in that little hole in the ground where the air didn't move and the sun beating on the dark-painted metal threatened to roast him alive. Ash gasped as he came back to himself and reality. He started the car and turned the air-conditioning on full blast. He needed cold, and he got plenty of it. Within minutes he was chilled and maybe shivering as frigid air flooded into the car. Ash ignored it as he put the car into gear. He pulled out of the parking space and drove through town without stopping. He didn't know where he was going to go. One thing was for sure: there was no way he could stay here. Brighton was with someone else, and running into him was only going to break Ash's heart and send him into a spin of despair that even now he wasn't sure he could recover from.

Ash saw the signs pointing to 15 and made the turn toward the freeway. That was his ticket out and away. He had to make a stop first, but he could do that. Then… well, maybe it was best if he went back to the hospital. He was a man of his word, unlike some people.

Fuck it all to hell if his lower lip didn't quiver just a little. Ash pounded the steering wheel with his hand. He hated that he was so fucking weak. He'd promised the doctors that there was something he had to do and that he'd come back. At the time Ash had meant it, even if in the back of his head he'd hoped that would be after a happy reunion with Brighton and….

Ash shook his head to clear away those thoughts and ended up swerving from one side of the road to the next. No, he needed to get it together long enough to see his aunt one more time and then drive back to the hospital. That was what he needed to do.

With his decision made, he got ready to turn his back on the one person he'd honestly expected would always be there for him.

CHAPTER 1

"YES, AUNT Petey. I'm on my way, and as soon as I get there, I'm going to get you out of that place and back home. You've worked hard and are much stronger than you were." Ash grinned into the phone. "I've been working on the house to get it ready for you." For weeks he'd come to Biglerville with what he needed in the back of the truck he'd traded the Taurus for—though sneaking in was more like it. Ash hadn't had the stomach to actually go into town or look around again. He knew Brighton Phillips was out there somewhere, and even after a year, he didn't think he was ready to see him again.

"I'm in the truck now, and I left the rehab center half an hour ago. I expect it will take me an hour or so to get there."

"Don't rush on my account," she said, though she sounded anxious and excited. "Is everything healed?"

"My leg is in a brace to give the bones support after the last surgery. But I can walk and get around just fine. They taught me what I need to know, and I can take it from here." He'd had to promise to find a physical therapy center there so he could continue his recovery. Thankfully it was his left leg, so he was able to drive.

"Am I going to be a burden?" Aunt Petey asked with fear in her voice.

"No." It was very likely she was going to be his salvation. "I rearranged the furniture in the house some, and what used to be Uncle Matt's office is going to be your bedroom. It has a closet, and the bathroom is just outside. A few weeks ago, some of my buddies brought down your furniture, so it looks a lot like your room upstairs, and you can close the door so, during the day, the

7

house will be just the way you like it. Give me a chance to get there, and we'll take care of everything."

"All right, sweetie. I love you." She hung up, and Ash closed his eyes just for a second—he was driving, after all.

Ash would have gone anywhere else, it didn't matter where, and leave Biglerville forever if not for his aunt. Over the last year, she had been his strength, nursing home or not. Without her, he would never have been able to pull his ass out of the spiral of depression that had gripped him. She gave him something and someone to live for.

He was nervous as hell about returning to Biglerville to live. There was no way he was going to be able to avoid Brighton forever. And hell, maybe that was the point. He had been special ops and had never shied away from anything in his life… but the last twenty-one months had knocked him on his ass again and again, and he was only now starting to feel like himself.

His leg ached by the time he arrived at the nursing home, and it took him a few minutes to get everything working and loosened up. Ash went inside and right down to his aunt's room. She was sitting on the side of her bed, a suitcase at the floor, her hands folded, as he walked inside.

"You said an hour." She turned to the clock. "You're ten minutes late." She broke into a smile as he bent down. She threw her arms around his neck and hugged the stuffing out of him. How a frail old lady had so much strength was beyond him, but she was happy, that was for sure, and that was also what mattered.

"I take it you're ready."

"Yes. I've been ready to kiss the backside of this place for months." She giggled, and Ash shook his head, still holding her. Aunt Petey was under five feet and weighed a hundred pounds soaking wet, but she was a force of nature. After she fell and broke her hip a year ago, everyone told him that was the end, that people her age who break hips never truly recovered. Other than going up and down stairs, Aunt Petey had beaten the odds, and now he was taking her home. That was a win for them both.

"Then let's go." He picked up the suitcase as he stood. "Is this all there is? You've been here a year."

"Honey, there is no way I'm bringing any of those frumpy death clothes home with me. I donated what I could and threw the rest of that junk away. I'm starting a new life, or at least I'm not going back to the way things were, so in a few days, you can take me shopping for some new clothes. I'm going for granny chic." She grinned. "You don't know any of those lady boys who could help, do you? I've been watching RuPaul, and I'd love for one of those gays to help. They have style."

Oh, good lord. Just what he needed, his aunt looking like a drag queen. "I don't, but I'm sure we can find someone." He let out a soft laugh as he helped her to her feet. He'd wondered if he'd need a wheelchair, but Aunt Petey did a little soft-shoe as she reached the door.

"Honey, I'm doing my own little dance of joy."

Ash took her arm to lead her out of the room and down the hall. His aunt said goodbye to everyone she passed with a grin and happy energy. To make this happen for her actually put a smile on Ash's lips, something he hadn't had in quite a while.

Once they were outside, he got his aunt into the truck and her things behind the seat before climbing in himself.

"Can we stop somewhere on the way home? I want one of Rose's cheeseburgers. Hell, I'd kill for anything that isn't bland, overcooked, or mushy." She turned to him and squeezed his arm. "It looks to me like you need to eat too. You've lost weight. You aren't going to catch any man's eye that skinny." She tsked softly.

"I've been in the hospital and rehab center. I had to watch what I ate, or I'd put on weight." He'd really been afraid that if he didn't slim down, his leg wouldn't be strong enough to carry him.

"Bullshit. You need to beef up like you were when you were in uniform." She sighed. "I fell in love with your uncle when he was in the Navy. He looked so gorgeous in his Navy blues... and even better out of them." She fanned herself, and Ash groaned.

"That's too much information."

"I'm just saying. If you want to catch a man, you need to have some bait." She looked him over again. "Sometimes you look so much like your uncle, it scares me."

"I know." He didn't want to take a bunch of trips down memory lane. Those paths all seemed to lead to only one place—or person—and he was trying to stay away from him. Ash pulled up in front of the Apple Diner, took the handicapped space, and placed the flip tag on the mirror.

"I hope that thing isn't for me." She opened the door and slowly slipped out. "I'm not ready for the grave or a special parking space."

The tag had been for her, but Ash was so grateful he had it. His leg throbbed and he wanted to sit down, put them both up, and maybe rest for a few hours. Instead, he kept quiet and followed her inside.

"Rose, honey," Aunt Petey called as the owner, who had to be nearly as old as his aunt, hurried out to hug her. "I told you I'd be back."

"That you did." Rose guided Aunt Petey to the nearest table. Of course, it would be the one right in the front bay window where they could be seen and he could see every single person on the street. He was tempted to ask for something else, but Aunt Petey was already sitting down and making herself comfortable, and he wasn't about to ask her to move.

"What can I bring you?" Rose asked.

"I want one of your cheeseburgers, with real bacon, and plenty of those waffle fries." She never opened the menu.

"What's your soup today?" Ash asked.

"Pffft... he'll have the same thing. I remember what you like, and don't even think of any of the soup and salad crap. We're celebrating my freedom. I feel like I've been sprung from the slammer. Oh, and bring us some of your special tea." She winked, and Ash was curious just what she was up to.

"Coming right up." Rose winked too, and Ash really started to wonder but said nothing. Truthfully, he was damn hungry, and the food sounded so good.

"Why are you looking anywhere but outside?"

"When did you get to be so nosey and pushy? What happened to the sweet aunt who always took care of me and saw to it that I had a chance to heal and grow up after Mom and Dad died? You were so kind and understanding then."

"I just spent a year with all those... old people. And let me tell you, in that place, pushy and nosey saved my ass more than once... and got me better food." She smiled and thanked Rose when she placed their glasses on the table.

The restaurant was slow, so Rose pulled up a chair and talked with his aunt. Ash tuned them out and took the chance to look around the diner, which hadn't changed since he was a kid. The counter was the same, with the soda fountain behind it. Heck, Rose could probably make a fortune if she decided to sell the place to a museum. Everything still said fifties, and it all still worked, which was amazing.

"Chester, take care of those glasses, would ya, hon?" Rose called.

"Sure, Gran," Chester said, hurrying over to pick up the tray.

Ash turned away just before the crash of glass shattered the peace of the restaurant.

His eyes were closed and he held his breath, waiting for the pain to bloom somewhere. He gripped the pipe in the dingy room and held on, knowing what was coming.

They wanted answers to questions he didn't have, but he wasn't able to convince them.

"Ash, sweetheart...."

Aunt Petey's voice cut through the noise in his head, and he opened his eyes. He was on the floor, clinging to the pole that held the table up, his chair overturned. Silverware and napkins littered

ANDREW GREY

the floor around him. Ash inhaled deeply, realizing he wasn't in that concrete room where his own screams came back at him again and again. He was home, in a diner.

"Sweetheart, it's all right." She sounded scared, and Ash carefully unwound his legs and righted the chair, then climbed into it while doing his best to stop the way his heart thudded in his chest.

"I'm fine." He scooted the chair back into place, and Rose got him fresh silverware and cleaned up the spilled water with a napkin without saying anything. He sipped his tea, then smacked his lips, trying to place the flavor. He wasn't sure what was in it, but the stuff tasted slightly buttery. He drank a little more before setting it aside once he placed the sickly-sweet scent. Special tea indeed.

"Rose, could I have a Coke, please?" He was starting to wonder what he was going to get after tasting that tea. Good lord, his aunt was going to get high as a kite off that stuff. Maybe it was good for her. Who was he to tell an eighty-year-old woman what she could and couldn't do, especially since he'd spent part of the last year self-medicating with alcohol and anything else he could find to try to keep the nightmares and flashbacks at bay. That and the fact that he was driving were why his tea would stay largely untouched. Ash didn't need to go back down that rabbit hole, no matter how enticing it might seem.

"Sure, honey." She smiled, took the cup of tea away, and came back with his Coke and their plates.

Ash turned away from the window and the two ladies as they talked, concentrating on his food and nothing else. It was part of how he'd learned to manage the demons that still lingered in him, waiting to burst out.

"Slow down, honey. No one is going to take it away from you."

He'd been shoveling waffle fries into his mouth but stopped, eating more slowly. As soon as the food hit his stomach, he'd been starving. He finished the fries and ate his burger, trying to

12

be polite, and the ladies talked on, his aunt eating quite a bit of her food.

"God, this is exactly what I needed."

"You should have called. I would have had Chester deliver food to the home for you. We do that occasionally." Rose smiled and stood, finishing her tea and taking the cup along with her. "You two have a nice lunch. I'm going to check on things. Holler if you need anything at all." She gently patted him on the shoulder as though she were saying she understood him, then walked into the kitchen.

"Do you have this special tea all the time?" Ash asked, eyebrow raised.

Aunt Petey rolled her eyes. "Sweetheart, I've been brewing and drinking special tea since long before you were born." She leaned over the table. "Who do you think taught her how to make it?" She raised her glass and sipped. "There is nothing like this to ease away the aches and pains of old age." She sighed. "I can't have more than one glass, but I feel almost like a teenager again." She smiled and returned to her food, eating all of her burger in cut-up pieces, then leaned back in her chair. "Now *that* was a lunch."

"You can't eat like that every day. It isn't good for you."

"Pffft," she countered, waving her hand. "I'm over eighty. How many years do I have left? And I can tell you that I have no intention of spending them eating mashed potatoes and drinking my meals through a straw or some such crap." She burped like a sailor and then giggled. "I'm going to the ladies' room. Ask Rose for the check when she comes back out, and we can go home." She stood and slowly made her way back to the restroom.

Ash sat quietly, his thoughts running in circles. He tried to steady them and turned to look out the window. The sun shone brightly, and he stared at passing cars. A shadow passed in front of his field of vision, and there he was, just like that, at the moment he'd been least prepared for it.

Brighton stood in front of the diner window, looking back the way he'd come. His hair was shorter, a lot of the curls shorn away, but Ash recognized him immediately. Brighton smiled as the man Ash had seen with Brighton a year ago walked up to him, holding the hand of a little girl of about five. Ash couldn't turn away as she raced to Brighton. He caught her, lifting her into his arms and twirling her into the air. Through the glass, he heard her muffled giggles.

Ash knew he should turn away and not torture himself, but Brighton looked so happy. He knew that smile and that laugh. He didn't even need to hear it; he knew exactly what it sounded like. The little girl stood on the sidewalk, taking each of their hands, and then the three of them continued down the sidewalk and out of his line of vision.

What the hell was Ash supposed to do now? He looked all around and pulled at the collar of his T-shirt, needing to breathe. He was back in the same small town where he'd grown up. He was going to see Brighton. Up until now he'd managed to stay away from the business district itself, doing what he needed to at the house and then leaving town. That wasn't going to be possible forever. But how the fuck was he supposed to see the man he still loved, the one who had ripped his heart out, with another man and a child? It was like they had the perfect family and he had nothing at all. Shit, he hardly knew who the fuck he was.

"Sweetheart?"

He barely heard his aunt as he stared out the window, desperate for another glimpse of the trio, but he didn't see them.

"Can you take me home?"

"Sure." He stood and went to the register to pay the bill, then guided his aunt outside and back to the truck.

"What are you looking for?" she asked, and Ash realized he'd been fixating on everyone on the sidewalk. "You saw him, didn't you?"

"Yes. I did. Brighton walked by the window, and I saw him with his perfect husband and family." He helped her into the truck

14

and gently closed the door. "It doesn't matter. I've seen him before, and there's nothing I can do about it." He had things he needed to do, and one of them was to get his aunt settled back at home, and he needed to get the hell off his feet before his leg screamed at him any louder for relief.

He got in the truck and headed out of town, still torturing himself by looking for Brighton.

"OH MY God," Aunt Petey squealed like a little girl as he pulled into the drive. "She looks so beautiful." She turned to him with a smile. "What did you do?"

"The house needed paint, and one of my friends, Casey, needed a job for a few weeks. He went a little wild, I think. He says the house was screaming to him as a painted lady, so that's what he did." Aunt Petey's old house was this large Victorian with a tower room high above the street that she had turned first into a playroom and then into Ash's sitting room. Now all the gingerbread stood out, painted shades of yellow and green.

"She looks like spring." Aunt Petey clapped her hands as she got out of the truck and walked slowly toward the front door. Ash followed with her things, and they went inside through the vestibule and then continued on to the living room. Aunt Petey turned, looking around. "What happened to my wallpaper?"

"It was peeling off the walls, so we removed it and then painted. I wanted something cheerful and something that would go with your furniture. Casey picked out the color, and I managed to paint this room for you." His arms had felt like they were going to fall off at the time, but he'd done it. "We also did the dining room, but in there Casey pulled the color from your wallpaper and it's now a pretty red. At least that's what he says." Ash set down the suitcase and escorted her into the dining room. She gasped and held his arm, tears flowing down her cheeks. He'd known she'd

15

love it, and the fact that her old house looked and felt fresh and vibrant had to be comforting for her. It had been for Ash.

"I love it." She patted his arm. "Go and put my things in the room you set up for me. I'm going to check out my kitchen." She walked slowly through the door, and Ash did as he was told, listening to the squeal. She was so happy, and that warmed Ash in a way nothing else had in months. "A new stove and a new icebox." She clapped her hands together, and Ash let her be, putting her things away and checking over her room one last time.

The walls were paneled in chestnut, and he'd hung family pictures and some of her paintings on each of the panels so she'd be surrounded by friends and family while she slept. Banging in the kitchen pulled him out of his thoughts.

"Aunt Petey, you don't need to be cooking right now." He returned to the living room and sat down, then put his legs up on a stool, sighing and closing his eyes as the pressure on his leg eased.

"Are you sure you don't want a snack?" Aunt Petey asked.

"We just ate. Come and sit down." He patted the nearby chair.

She took a seat and put a hand on his arm. "What's that? It's huge." She pointed, and Ash reached for the remote to turn on the sixty-inch high-definition television screen.

"I got cable with all the channels, so you'll have plenty to watch." He grinned. There was no denying he'd bought the television for himself. He liked his TV and wanted to be able to watch the games in comfort.

"Good lord." She sat back as the screen came to life. "This isn't one of those compensation things, is it?" Leave it to Aunt Petey.

Ash snickered. "No. Now, if I come home with a Corvette, you'll definitely know I'm compensating." He laughed, and she did right along with him. He changed the channel until he found something he thought she might like, then rested his head back. "If I scream or yell in my sleep, don't come near me. Make noise if you want, but stay away. Sometimes I grab at people because I'm still in my dreams, and they're not good ones."

"Do you have PTSD?"

"Yes, and lots of flashbacks and stuff like that, especially when I sleep." He didn't like to talk about it, but she had to know.

Aunt Petey nodded and turned back to the television. "What did they do to you?"

He shook his head. Ash had no intention of talking about that. He got through that hell because of his aunt and his memories of Brighton. They had been his rocks, his touchstones, invisible companions he'd clung to when he was in so much pain that he prayed to die. He couldn't share that with the folks he loved because that would tarnish them, and he never wanted to do that. In a way it would be like letting his torturers win, and that was something he could never live with.

Ash closed his eyes, sighing, avoiding the question. He'd gotten quite good at that, even in the hospital. The doctors and therapists had pressed him a few times, but he'd kept quiet and intended to for the rest of his life. He let his breathing even out and started to fall asleep. Sometimes he was afraid of what his mind would conjure up when given free rein, but he was very tired, and just sitting helped the ache in his leg dissipate. There were times when he felt so damn old.

"Do you remember how you used to play in this room?" Aunt Petey asked.

"Uh-huh," Ash answered without opening his eyes.

"You had that video game console, and you used to sit in front of it all the time with the volume low so I wouldn't tell you to stop." She seemed so happy, and Ash didn't want to discourage her.

"I remember," he said quietly. Though he tried not to, because one of his playmates at the time had been a smaller boy, Brighton. They'd been friends since Ash came to live with his aunt. That first year had been misery on top of sadness after his mom and dad's

17

deaths. "What I loved most was that you used to let me have fun as long as I didn't break anything and cleaned up when I was done." Those had been the only rules. He sighed and drifted on waves of gentle memories. Maybe this was what he needed, to come back home where he knew he'd been loved. His muscles relaxed as the old movie about baseball and a cat on television slowly grew more distant.

The oak tree out back loomed overhead with ropes that hung down from the platform he was building. Ash stood under the great green expanse, looking up at the thick canopy.

"Are you going to look up or climb up?" Brighton asked, grabbing the nearest rope and propelling himself upward with the ease of a monkey. He was always climbing something.

"I'll beat you one day." Ash grabbed for the nearest rope and climbed as well, reaching the platform a second before Brighton. He stood up in the branches. "See, I told you."

"Yeah, yeah." Brighton pulled on the other rope, raising the box of tools they'd loaded. The plan had been to build a treehouse, but they'd only gotten the platform finished. "We need to get to work if we're ever going to get this done."

They started building the first wall that would eventually be raised along one side, which in Ash's mind morphed into the completed treehouse.

The now-teenaged Brighton was sitting on the floor of the treehouse. It seemed to have gotten smaller as they'd gotten older, but neither of them cared.

"I hate math," Brighton groused as he passed over the book so Ash could look at the problem.

"It's not that hard. Just move things to the same side of the equation and then solve it." Ash moved closer, sitting next to him, showing Brighton how to do it, and then waited while Brighton finished the work, doing it correctly. "Perfect." Ash smiled, and Brighton did the same, his eyes widening as he looked at him. Ash's heart beat faster and his cheeks heated. Brighton leaned a little

closer, and Ash drew in, pulled by a force he didn't understand, until he kissed Brighton, or Brighton kissed him—he wasn't sure and it didn't matter.

Pain instantly ripped through him as the image faded from his mind. Ash did his best to hold on to it like a lifeline. He clenched his hands together, willing Brighton to stay with him.

"I have nothing to tell you," Ash said for the millionth time. "I don't know anything about that."

Ash was yanked away from the pole, and he stumbled before his head was plunged into a tub of icy water. He held his breath, and fingers gripped his hair, forcing him under, holding him there. The images of Brighton grew stronger as Ash willed them to let him die. This needed to be over. There wasn't much more he could take. Once again he held on to Brighton as though he were tangible, giving him strength and support. Darkness closed around him, and he thought this might finally be the end.

Ash gasped and sat upright, blinking, hands flailing. He came in contact with the lamp and pulled it onto his lap. It was only a dream. The baseball movie once again came forward, and he saw the walls of the living room. He took a deep breath to calm his thumping heart and set the lamp back on the table next to him.

Aunt Petey turned and looked at him. Ash expected fear, but what he saw was understanding. "Does that happen a lot?" she asked.

"Sometimes. When I'm asleep, I have no control over the dreams and—" He wasn't going to go into their content and how his mind had mixed the happy with the terror to spoil some of the best and kindest memories he had, mixing them with nightmares until he couldn't bear to think of either one. Talk about pollution.

"What can I do to help?" That was the aunt he knew and loved. Her first thought wasn't for herself or her safety, living with someone who couldn't seem to control himself part of the time, but for him and what he needed.

"I've seen so many doctors, I don't know what to do any longer. They don't seem to help. I had one who was able to explain what was happening to me, and he tried to give me some skills so I could begin to cope with what happened. Mostly they all said that, over time, the nightmares would fade and become less powerful. One doctor said that the best way I could get past this was to make some new memories to overlay these." He put his feet on the floor and slowly stood.

"What do you think?" Aunt Petey asked. "That sounds like a bunch of bullshit to me. Something they'd say when they don't have an answer."

"Because they don't. They did offer to give me a bunch of drugs and things to try to help me, but all those did was make me sleep sixteen hours a day and not give a shit about anything. I stopped taking them and could think again." He got tired of being a guinea pig. "Do you want something to drink?"

"No, honey. I'm fine," she answered. "Good God! Can't that idiot even catch the ball? He gets paid millions." Aunt Petey sure hadn't changed a bit. She always said she didn't care for sports but seemed to know everything about what was happening.

He went into the kitchen and poured a glass of grape juice from the refrigerator. He'd bought some beer, and though he wanted one, he went for the juice instead. He returned to the living room, where Aunt Petey had found the remote and was surfing through the channels.

"How can there be so many programs and all of them are complete shit?" She continued flipping and found where someone was running *Moonstruck.* "Have you seen this?"

"I can't remember. I don't think so," he said, watching the opening credits.

"Then let's watch. I love it when Cher smacks Nicolas Cage." She leaned back, making herself comfortable.

Ash needed something to watch so he didn't fall back to sleep. That was another thing they'd taken from him—sleep was something he feared now. During the day, he could keep his mind on what he wanted, most of the time. But when he was asleep…. What hurt most was the way his memories got so mixed up and what should have been happy was twisted and warped.

"You know, maybe you need to meet some new people."

"Maybe." What he really needed was a way to put the shattered pieces of his heart back together. For a year he'd worked on trying to get his head together. But his heart… that was a completely different matter.

CHAPTER 2

"UNCLE BRIGHTON!" his niece, Violet, called as she ran down the sidewalk. "Look what I drew for you."

He lifted her into his arms, twirling her up into the air, listening to her happy giggles. They'd been a long time in coming, and it lightened Brighton's heart to hear them.

"Were you a good girl in school today?" Brighton asked, setting her back on her feet.

"Yes," she answered, taking Brighton's hand as his cousin Raymond walked up to join them.

Brighton raised his gaze and smiled. "Thank you for picking her up."

"It was no problem. She and I had ice cream, and we were just going inside so she could get some chocolate."

Sometimes Raymond was an evil man.

"You're trying to get her hyped up on sugar. What did I ever do to you?" Brighton teased, though he led Violet back inside the store to the candy counter. He let her pick out one thing, and Raymond paid for it. "You have to wait until after dinner to eat it."

"Okay, Uncle Brighton." She smiled, her eyes huge, and dang it, he knew she was already working to get what she wanted. This kid was going to drive the boys crazy when she got older.

"I mean it, and don't give me that look. I know it works with Uncle Raymond, but you can't have the candy bar until dessert." Brighton took her hand, and she held the small bag with her candy in her other one. He looked over at Raymond. "Do you have plans for tonight? You could join Violet and me for dinner."

"Thanks, but I have a date tonight." Raymond grinned as they walked down the sidewalk. "After work, I stopped in at the library, and there was a guy in there. He was checking out the videos and he kept looking at me, so I ambled over and asked him a few questions. He asked if I wanted to get some coffee tonight." He practically floated as they walked.

"Swing me!" Violet said. She handed her bag to Brighton and then took Raymond's hand and jumped into the air. They swung her back and forth as they walked, Violet squealing as she dangled in the air.

"Of course you'd pick up a guy in the library," Brighton said, lifting Violet once again. "I didn't know there were that many gay people in town, but leave it to you to find them."

"You could too if you stopped living like a monk."

"What's a monk?" Violet asked.

"Your Uncle Brighton," Raymond answered, chuckling.

"Is it like a monkey?" she pressed, and Raymond knelt down, pulling Violet in his arms.

"You're my monkey," Raymond said as he stood, twirling her in circles. Brighton sighed, watching the two of them. It was nice that they were happy. He just wished he could feel the same way. Raymond reached over to pat his shoulder before turning to Violet. "Let's get you home."

Brighton lifted his gaze as the sky darkened and the breeze picked up, carrying a hint of moisture and a definite chill. Two blocks later they opened the door and climbed up the stairs to their tiny apartment. Well, it was only tiny because of the three of them living there. Officially it was a two-bedroom apartment, but he and Raymond had managed to turn a small alcove off the living room into a third bedroom with a room divider and tall dresser for Violet. Her door was a curtain made from pink fabric that Violet picked out herself. She thought it was cool and seemed happy, which was all that mattered.

Violet went right to her room and put away her backpack while Brighton headed to the kitchen to start making dinner. Raymond disappeared into his room and closed the door.

"Can I watch TV?" Violet bounded in, and Brighton got her the remote. She climbed onto the sofa and turned on the TV to find a cartoon on the Disney Channel.

"You know, you need to get out once in a while," Raymond said as he came out of his bedroom. "Do you realize it's been eighteen months since they told you about Ash? He's gone and isn't coming back, and you need to find someone to share your life." He leaned closer. "And don't say that's what you have me and Violet for. You need someone to love and love you in return."

"I had that once, and I don't know if I can ever have that again." Brighton knew what it felt like to have someone who was the other half of him. "Besides, Violet is still settling in and I need to concentrate on her. Allie asked me to take care of Violet if anything ever happened to her, and I intend to do the very best that I can." He knew the answer was a cop-out of sorts and that he was hiding behind his niece, but he wasn't ready to date yet. "So you go on out and have a good time." He did a double take on Raymond's outfit. He wore a pair of jeans that had to be two sizes too small and a shirt that showed off his arms. "Where are you going?"

"To Rose's for coffee."

"Don't you think you're a little overdressed… or underdressed, in this case? God, you don't want to cut off circulation to your bits. And this is Biglerville."

"The guy I'm dating is from LA. His name is Ethan, and he's Justin Hawthorne's assistant. So he's used to being around people who are really cool and interesting and…." Raymond shifted his gaze to the floor.

"You are not allowed to be unsure of yourself. Go back in there and change. Let this Ethan see who you really are and he's sure to like you. And if he doesn't, I'll show up at his house and kick his ass." Brighton pulled Raymond into his arms. "Now go ahead and change. Just be yourself."

With a smile, Raymond went back into his room while Brighton returned to making dinner.

"Violet, please turn that down a little."

She lowered the volume, and Brighton cut up some lettuce to make them each a small salad. He was really blessed that Violet loved vegetables, though if he asked her what she wanted to eat she'd tell him bacon. That girl would eat bacon for each and every meal if he let her. He opened the door to the refrigerator and pulled out some chicken he'd already cooked and began cutting it into small pieces, along with a little celery and some herbs, as well as chopped nuts.

"Is this better?" Raymond asked, and Brighton nodded.

"You look great. The slacks are nicer than the tight jeans, and I like that shirt. The green is great on you." Brighton watched as Raymond pulled on his shoes and got ready to go. "Take an umbrella. You're going to need it."

Raymond looked out the front window, groaning as the rain lashed the glass.

Lightning flashed and thunder rumbled, sending Violet off the sofa and into his arms. He set aside what he was doing, lifted her up, and took her back to the sofa. "It's just thunder. There's nothing to be afraid of." He sat down with Violet on his lap and turned to Raymond. "Just wait a little while. This isn't going to last long. When are you supposed to be there?"

Raymond checked his phone. "Fifteen minutes." He shoved it back in his pocket. "The one time I'm ready early and I'm stuck waiting until the storm lets up."

Brighton patted Violet's knee. "Why don't you go get the really big umbrella for Uncle Raymond? That way he won't get wet." He smiled as Violet hurried to the closet and brought over the black-and-white umbrella. She jumped when the thunder rolled again, but handed it to Raymond and then sat next to Brighton once more. "Do you think you can sit here while I finish making you something to eat?" He tweaked her nose, and she nodded slowly.

The storm was already moving on and the thunder sounded less sharp. Raymond took the umbrella and headed for the door to the stairs. "I'll see you later." He waved, and Violet waved back. Raymond closed the door behind him, and Brighton stood to return to the kitchen.

Violet laughed as one of the characters on her show did something funny. He adored that sound. She'd been with him for six months now. His sister had developed cancer, and by the time they diagnosed it, she was beyond help and lasted only a few more weeks. The strain she'd had was nasty and had left none of her untouched. At the end she'd been little more than skin and bones. One of the hardest things Brighton had ever had to do was take Violet home with him as she cried for her mother while he was barely able to hold himself together. Thank God Raymond had come to stay with him the year before.

Just like when Ash walked out of his life for the last time to take his assignment. Ash had promised it would be his last one, that his time was up after that. It all turned out to be true, though not in the way either of them had hoped at the time. When he'd seen on the news that men were missing and that nine of them hadn't survived, Brighton hadn't believed it. Weeks went by, and then months of despair. He heard nothing, and by the time Raymond came to stay with him, he was a complete basket case. Raymond had helped him get back on his feet and start living again, and he'd been there through it all when Allie had told him she was sick and requested he raise Violet for her.

Brighton put down his knife and turned away, not wanting Violet to see the tears welling in his eyes. He still missed both Ash and Allie. But at least with his sister, he had the best part of her and would for the rest of his life. Brighton's mother and father had said they wanted to raise Violet, but Allie had asked him, and he wasn't about to give her up. He needed her just as much as she needed him.

"Can I watch another show?" Violet asked, and Brighton nodded.

"Sure, honey." Sometimes this felt so overwhelming for him. More than once he'd wondered if he'd done the right thing. Maybe Violet would be better off with his mom and dad, but they… dang it, they were so repressive—that was the best way to describe it. Allie had raised Violet with love and encouragement, not a million rules to show who had authority and power. Brighton was determined to bring Violet up the way Allie would have, with all the love he could muster. The fucking hard part was that his heart was still in pieces.

Brighton went back to work, finishing up dinner and making a plate for Violet. He brought over the footstool and let her use it as a table. Violet watched her program and ate, attention riveted on the television. Brighton observed her closely. When she'd come to live with him, Violet had helped repair his damaged heart. She hadn't healed it, but at least she'd shown him that it wasn't dead completely.

"Can we go to Disney World sometime?" she asked, turning away from one of the myriad commercials for the theme parks that ran over and over.

He wanted to be able to take her and do all the things that other kids her age did, but they didn't have the money. Brighton worked for a little over minimum wage, and he got Social Security for Violet, so he had enough to care for her. His sister had had some life insurance, but Brighton had put all that money away for Violet so she'd have the chance to go to college someday. He was determined that she would have the opportunities that he never had.

"I hope so, sweetheart," Brighton told her. Maybe if he could save a little each month and put it away, then he could afford to take her. They'd have to drive back and forth because the cost of plane tickets was out of the question, but he could probably make it happen if Raymond was able to come with them and help with defraying some of the cost and driving. "I'll try to see what I can do. Someday we'll go." His parents would probably love to take her down there, and maybe he should ask to see if that was something they wanted to do.

"Okay." Violet turned back to the television as the program returned, and she went back to eating. Thankfully his answer had been good enough for her, because it was the best one he had.

Brighton made himself a plate and used the few minutes of quiet as his chance to have dinner. Once they were done eating, Violet handed him her plate, and Brighton took it along with his to the kitchen. She'd eaten everything he'd given her, so Brighton gave her half the candy bar she'd gotten earlier. He didn't want her eating that much sugar, and she seemed happy with it. Brighton wrapped up the rest of it for her treat the following day.

"You can watch this program, and then it's bath time and you need to go to bed. I'll read you a story, but no whining or crying, okay?" Bedtime had never been an issue, but lately she'd decided that whining and acting up would get her what she wanted. It worked sometimes with Raymond, but Brighton wasn't going to allow it.

"Okay." She sat next to him, and Brighton put his arm around her. They watched whatever show she'd been enthralled in for the next half hour. It was something set in a school with know-it-all children, not that he paid attention to it. He was more interested in the way Violet laughed and giggled while she watched their antics.

When the credits started, Brighton put any pleading to rest by turning off the television, taking her hand, and leading Violet to the bathroom. He got the water running at just the right temperature and added her toys and some bubbles. She undressed and climbed in the tub, and Brighton let her bathe and play while he took care of her clothes and located a nightgown and underwear for her. When he returned, Brighton washed her hair and made sure she washed everywhere before turning on the shower. She didn't want to take one, but she liked rinsing off that way, and as soon as she was soap-free, he wrapped her in a big, fluffy towel so she wouldn't be cold.

Violet stood still as he let the water out and grabbed another towel to dry her hair. Then he let her get dressed for bed and brushed her hair. She brushed her teeth, and then they raced to bed. Violet won, and Brighton got her settled under the covers, turned the lights low, and opened *Curious George*. It was one of his favorites, and thankfully Violet loved it too.

He read the story, and Violet's eyes were drooping almost before he finished. Closing the book, he glanced at Violet, got up carefully so he didn't wake her, and turned out the light. He placed the book on the shelf in the corner and left her room, pulling the curtain.

As quietly as he could, Brighton did the dishes, then turned out all the lights on his way to his room, where he lay propped up on the bed, turned on his television, and tried to find something to watch. There was nothing interesting on, so he read for a while and then got ready for bed himself.

As he returned to his bedroom, the picture beside the bed caught his eye. Ash smiled out of the frame, with Brighton in his arms, legs up, arms around Ash's neck. The whole thing had been a joke, and a friend of his had snapped the picture just after Ash had literally swept him off his feet. Everyone told him he should put the pictures he had of Ash away and do his best to put that behind him. But he couldn't. How many people found the person they were meant to be with at twelve? He was friends with Ash, had his first kiss with Ash, and after that never wanted anyone else. Sure, they had been separated when Ash went into the service. But Ash had always come back, with stories, but mostly just as much in love as when he left. Ash had been nearing the end of his tour of duty, and the two of them had made plans for when he came back.

"Uncle Brighton," Violet said, standing in his doorway.

"What is it, honey?" He set the picture on the nightstand as she raced forward and propelled herself onto the bed.

"Who is that?" She pointed to the picture.

"It's a friend of mine. He's gone, like your mommy is gone." He pulled her into a hug. "Let's get you back into bed."

"There are ghosts." She'd been afraid of shadows lately.

"Come on. I'll sit with you and keep the ghosts away while you fall back to sleep." He carried her to bed and tucked her in. She rolled over and, after a few minutes, fell right to sleep. This time he remembered to turn on her rainbow night-light and then quietly left her room.

Brighton was exhausted, and he knew Raymond would be quiet when he came home. Brighton's days began early, getting Violet ready for preschool. In his room he climbed back into his own bed. His dreams were as close as he could get to Ash, and as time passed, Ash came to him less frequently. But it was all he had, and the thought of losing him forever was too much. Yeah, he knew that he was being dumb and should move on, but he couldn't. If he let Ash go, then he'd truly be gone, and a world without his best friend, protector, and lover was one he didn't want to be part of.

"YOU LET me sleep in," Brighton said the following morning when he came out for breakfast. Violet sat at the table with a bowl of cereal, dressed in some god-awful pants-and-shirt combination that nearly hurt his eyes.

"You seemed content." Raymond must have followed his gaze. "She picked out her own clothes." He raised his hands in surrender, and Brighton smiled. Violet loved her bright colors.

"I guessed that." He bent down, giving Violet a big, wet kiss that left her giggling. "What time did you get in?" Brighton poured himself a small glass of juice. They could only afford so much, and he mostly left it for Violet to have in the mornings.

"A little after eleven. Ethan was a really nice guy. He lives in LA and is here with Justin Hawthorne's mother. She wanted to see some friends and Justin is busy, so Ethan brought her back." Raymond cleared away Violet's empty dishes. "Go ahead and get your backpack. The bus will be here in ten minutes."

Violet stared ahead, her eyes glassy and her brow wrinkled. Brighton placed his hand on her forehead. She looked a little flushed and felt hot. He turned to Raymond. "Go get the children's Tylenol, and I'll call the school to let them know that she's sick."

"Uncle Brighton…." She screwed up her face, and Brighton lifted her in his arms and headed to the bathroom. They made it in time, and the poor thing lost her breakfast. She whined, and Brighton got her a small drink of water before carrying her to her bed.

"Do you need me to stay with her?" Raymond asked.

"No. Today was my day off. So go on to work, and I'll stay here with her." He had a million things he needed to do, but Violet was more important, and hopefully while she slept, he could do a few chores. He gently lay her down and found some pajamas for her. Violet didn't protest as he got her clothes off, helped her into her pajamas, and got her into bed.

Raymond brought her the children's Tylenol, and after he gave her a little, Violet settled down. "Does your tummy hurt?" Raymond asked, stroking her forehead.

"Yes."

"Are you going to be sick again?" Brighton asked, but she shook her head, closing her eyes. "Good. Uncle Raymond is going to get you some Sprite, and after you wake up, you can sit with me and we'll watch television." He soothed her back down, and she was already closing her eyes. Brighton left the little room with Raymond, biting his lower lip.

"She's going to be okay. There's something going around. The school said that a lot of the kids are coming down with it." Raymond patted him on the shoulder to reassure him, then hurried to his room and returned with his pack slung over his shoulder. "I'll run and get the soda and be right back." Raymond took off, and Brighton finished cleaning up the dishes and then got the laundry together even though it was going to have to wait. He couldn't leave Violet to run to the laundromat.

Raymond returned with the soda and some crackers. He hurried back out, and for the millionth time, Brighton was grateful for his cousin's support. After Ash left, Brighton had retreated from everyone to wait out the time and count the days until his return. But the months went by, and then—after determining that Ash was gone—he had to somehow pick up the pieces, but he hadn't been able to do it alone. Thankfully, Raymond had come to live with Brighton and hadn't left.

Knowing he needed to be quiet and stay close, Brighton went to his room and to his closet, searching for a box he'd put out of sight a while ago. It took him a few minutes to find it, but he hauled it out and set it on the bed. He hesitated and then opened the flaps, carefully searching for the album he wanted. He pulled it out, closed the box again, and put it back where he'd found it. Brighton wasn't ready to go through the rest of what was in there.

He took the album and went to the living room to sit on the sofa. He loved this sofa. If he sat at the one end, it was perfect for watching television, but the other was near the window and he could look outside. Brighton sat near the bay window and opened the album. Ash's aunt Petey had started this for him when he was a kid. As far as he knew, she'd made one for Ash as well, and she probably still had that one. He opened the cover and immediately his twelve-year-old self, with Ash's arm around his shoulders, smiled out at him. They had been swimming at one of the lakes and their hair was plastered to their heads. Brighton couldn't help smiling. The memory of that day was no longer clear, except for Ash's energy. He turned the page, smiling once again.

One of Aunt Petey's Easter egg hunts, which were legendary. Brighton and Ash colored dozens of eggs, and Aunt Petey hid them and all kinds of other things—mugs, candy, toys, even wrapped presents. Granted, those were usually clothes, but they were always fun things and stuff he'd needed for school.

That woman…. Brighton leaned back, closing his eyes as he looked up toward the ceiling, keeping the tears at bay. He should have kept closer to her. She'd been through just as much pain as he had. Brighton had visited Aunt Petey before she went to the nursing home, and she'd been so frail. He made a note to find out where she was and go see her again.

Brighton turned his attention back to the album, grinning like he and Ash were as they held up their baskets full of loot. Damn. He set the album aside and turned toward the window, staring outside. Every time he took a trip down memory lane, the trips centered around one person. There was no escaping it. Ash had been a part of his life for so long that…. Maybe it was best to leave the past where it was.

Cars drove down the wide main street of town, mostly heading south toward the tourist mecca of Gettysburg. Some pulled into spaces and parked, and people walked up or down the sidewalk to get where they were going.

A figure caught his attention. It was slightly hunched and walking with a limp. He leaned closer to the glass, and his eyes widened. That man… he…. Brighton's throat went dry. That man looked like Ash. His hair was longer and he was limping, but the shoulders and the way he…. Brighton's heart beat faster and he leaned closer, watching, trying to see if his eyes were deceiving him.

Brighton stood and hurried toward the stairs just as Violet called for him.

"Uncle Brighton, I'm thirsty."

He turned back to the window, looking for the man once more, but didn't see him. He turned both ways to see as far as he could, but the man was gone, if he'd ever been there in the first place. Brighton blinked and shook his head, leaving the window to go to Violet's room. He got her up and gently carried her into the living room, then settled her with pillows and a blanket on the sofa.

"I'm going to get you a little soda." He got a cup and poured half an inch of Sprite in it and returned to where Violet lay. "Just drink a little and see how your tummy is."

She drank a few sips, and he took the cup back and set it on the table. Brighton turned on the television, finding something appropriate for her to watch. He hoped she'd go back to sleep for a while, but she seemed awake and much more alert. Brighton left her watching television so he could make his bed and clean up the room and bathroom before returning to the living room to check on Violet and look out the window.

He checked the rest of the morning and all afternoon, constantly looking out at the sidewalk to where he'd seen Ash, though as the day went on, he realized he was being silly. Some guy had looked like Ash from forty feet away. It didn't mean anything. He'd been looking at pictures and thinking of him, so his mind imprinted Ash's characteristics on someone else. That was the only explanation that didn't have him going crazy.

The door below opened and closed, followed by footsteps on the stairs. He expected Raymond to come in, so he didn't anticipate the knock. He got up and answered the door.

"Hi, Mom," he said gently, stepping back. "Violet didn't go to school because she isn't feeling well," he warned her before she stepped inside.

"Raymond called. I was hoping to see her," she said excitedly, pressing a bag of groceries in his arms. "I brought a few things for the both of you." She turned to Violet. "Hi, honey," she said softly. "Are you feeling better?"

"Yes. Uncle Brighton gave me Sprite." She went into his mother's arms, and he carried the groceries into the kitchen to put them away. He sighed and said nothing as he pulled out boxes of frozen stuff. Brighton spent extra to help make sure Violet had the best diet he could give her. He had been brought up on fast food and frozen, reheated everything because his mother had never learned to cook.

"Do you want me to read you a story?" his mother asked.

Brighton set down the groceries and brought over some books from Violet's room. He turned off the television so she could hear. Then he finished putting things away while his mother read Violet to sleep. Once she was quiet on the sofa, curled up under the blanket, his mother joined him in the kitchen.

"You know, your father and I could provide so much more for her." She turned toward Violet's room. "She could have a real room with a door and...."

"Mom. Allie asked me to raise her, and I will do my very best. Violet likes her room and she's happy. So just let her be. You and Dad are retired and have your own lives." Brighton didn't add that if they took her away, he was likely to completely fall apart.

"There's nothing more important than my granddaughter." He hated that haughty attitude, like her ideas were the only ones that mattered. "And she needs both a mother and a father figure in her life, and...."

"Stop it, mother. I know how you feel about me. You made that very clear when I was a teenager. But I'm not stepping aside in favor of you and Dad. Allie asked me to care for Violet, and I'm going to honor her wishes." He needed something to do. He turned away and opened the refrigerator to get out some tea. He got some glasses, poured the tea, and pressed one into his mother's hand.

She barely paid attention, watching where Violet slept. "But I don't understand why she'd pick you over us."

"Mom. She saw the way you treated me when you found out I was different. What if Violet is different, like me? Are you going to be able to handle that? No kid should be forced to try to be someone they aren't because you're uncomfortable with anyone who doesn't fit your idea of right and wrong." He sniffed as he remembered the uproar when his mother had found some magazines he'd thought he'd hidden really well. There had been yelling and threats, and when he didn't back down, and told them he was gay, his mother hadn't talked to him for nearly a week. Of course he'd run to Ash, and Brighton had stayed in one of the rooms at Aunt Petey's for a few weeks until his parents came around a little.

"That isn't going to happen. She's a girl. And we pretend all the time, so…." She paused and sipped from her glass.

"No one should have to pretend, Mom. That's the point, and you don't get it. You barely talked to Allie when she told you she was pregnant and had no intention of marrying the father because he turned out to be a complete jackass. You still pressured her to do it. Thankfully she told you where to go and did things on her own."

Jack had turned into an even bigger jackass and skipped the state when he was awarded no custody and visitation but ordered to pay child support. The scum.

"Okay." She set her glass on the counter. "I don't want to fight you."

"Then don't. Just be there for Violet. She needs her grandma and grandpa. Be the best ones you can, because she isn't going to be little like this for very long." He smiled. "Violet asked me last night if we could go to Disney sometime. I think she's too young now, but in a few years, it would be fun to take her."

"Then you should." His mother smiled, and Brighton smiled back. "And I agree that you should wait till she's older." She looked around, tapping her fingers on the glass, humming just under her breath.

Brighton knew that routine very well. "What is it, Mom?"

"I'm just wondering how things will be when you meet… when you… well… have a friend." She continued tapping her glass.

"First thing, Violet already knows I'm gay and what it means because Uncle Raymond had a… friend… once and she saw him kiss his… friend. She asked, and we told her that you kiss the people you care about. She understood, and that was the end of it. Things aren't that different, not really, and once you teach children to accept other people, they do." He finished his tea and put the glass in the sink and the pitcher back in the refrigerator. "You and Dad did your best. I know that, and I don't blame you or hold anything against you. I've learned in the last few months that there are no manuals to being a parent. You do what you think is best, and that's what I'm trying to do. It's what you and Dad did."

"We tried."

"Then support me and don't put up barriers or look down on where we live. All that matters is that Violet is loved and cared for above everything and everyone else. She has me and she has Raymond. I want her to know that she has you and Dad too."

"Of course she does." She patted his hand, and Brighton looked up from the table. "And so do you. Really. Your dad and I... we don't understand... but that doesn't mean we don't love you."

"I know, Mom. Everything has been really hard." He stood and leaned against her. To his surprise, she hugged him tightly. It had been a long time since she'd done that. "I still miss him, Mom."

"Who?"

"Ash. I know you don't understand, but he was the one. The other half of my heart." He kept his face pressed to her blouse because he didn't want to see her expression, but he had to talk to someone, and before... well, before shit fell apart, she had always listened.

"That was...."

"I know, Mom. He left almost two years ago, but I still miss him."

"He was your friend," his mother said, rubbing his back.

"No, Mom. He was my heart and everything. When things got bad, he was the one who was always there. He loved me, and I loved him." He raised his head, wiping his eyes. "Do you remember how you felt about Dad when you married him, like he was perfect and the greatest man you'd ever met?"

She nodded. "Your dad was something else then."

"Well, that's how I felt about Ash. We were going to build a life together. We'd even picked out a house we wanted to buy together." He held his mother tighter. "I know you think I'm stupid and that things between two men can't work out, but...."

His mother cradled his head gently. "Sweetheart, you can do anything you set your mind to." Her voice cracked slightly. "Did you really love him?"

Brighton nodded. "He was everything to me, and I haven't figured out how to really move on." He swallowed and slowly moved out of his mother's arms. "But I have to. This has gone on too long, and I need to get my head together and screwed on straight for Violet." He shook his head. "Enough of this foolishness. Ash is gone, and I can't wallow in this anymore." He went over to check on Violet, who was still asleep. He kissed her forehead and found it much cooler than it had been earlier. "Do you need to go right away?"

"No. I have time."

"I need to do some laundry. It's just down the street, and I can't leave her."

"Of course I can stay." She took her tea and sat in the chair nearest Violet.

Brighton got the bag of laundry and his supplies before thanking his mother and hurrying down the stairs and a block over to the laundromat. Luckily it was quiet and he was able to sort everything into three machines and get them all started.

"Hi, sweetie," Louise said as she came out of the back room. "You're here late."

"Violet is sick, and my mom is sitting with her." He sat down and picked up one of the magazines to read while he waited.

"I can watch things for you. The wash takes thirty minutes. If you want to go sit with Violet, just come on back then." She smiled, and he put the magazine aside.

He left the baskets on top of the machines and pushed the door open, turning to wave his thanks. When he turned toward home, he nearly bumped into a man and looked up to apologize, staring into the pair of eyes that he'd seen in his dreams for months.

"I'm sorry." He closed his eyes, shaking his head, certain he was seeing things.

"Brighton."

He'd know that voice anywhere.

Brighton stopped once again, turning slowly. "It's you." He gasped as he blinked to make sure he wasn't seeing things. "What? How? When?" His mouth went dry. "I thought you…. How did…." He kept stammering every time he opened his mouth, his heart soaring to the clouds. He nearly jumped for joy until the other shoe fell and a realization washed over him. Ash was alive and had been for a year and a half of pain and loss. Maybe Ash…. Anger warred with relief and then overwhelmed it.

"You… you…. Where the fuck have you been? I waited for months and thought you were dead, and you…." He was so angry and yet on the verge of tears. Ash was alive and standing in front of him, and he wasn't sure what to think. He'd dreamed of this day for the last year and a half, and now he had what he wanted. But until this moment he'd never contemplated what his return could mean.

Ash took a step back, looking uncertain. "I…."

"I thought you were dead." Brighton stepped closer, thrusting out his chest. "They said that no one returned from your last mission. And now, not only aren't you dead, but it's been months and months and you didn't come back to me." His hands shook. He wasn't going to stand here and cry in front of Ash. He'd been carrying a torch for him, and fuck it all if he'd been alive and hadn't bothered to come back. Jesus, Brighton thought his heart had broken when he thought Ash was dead, but being rejected like this shattered it into little pieces. Everything he'd been hoping for was a lie.

"I wasn't dead, as you can see," Ash said, the hurt in his eyes draining away, replaced with resignation and something Brighton couldn't read, but it might have been defeat. "Aw hell, it doesn't matter." He stepped out of the way and continued down the street, slowly walking away.

Brighton watched him, his anger melting as Ash turned the corner. It wasn't until he was out of sight that Brighton's anger evaporated and his legs nearly buckled from under him. What the hell had he done? Brighton turned, hurrying to where Ash had gone, but when he turned the corner, he couldn't find him.

A truck pulled away from the curb just ahead of him and sped off, most likely carrying Ash from him once again.

Brighton swore as he realized he'd blown his chance at what he'd been wanting ever since the day that Ash had left. "Fucking hell." He turned away, tears filling his eyes.

Ash was alive and he'd stayed away. Brighton's heart broke all over again at the realization that Ash hadn't truly cared for him. That was almost harder to bear than losing Ash in the first place. With not enough time left to return home as he'd intended, Brighton trudged slowly back toward the laundromat, wishing he could climb into one of the machines and hide to lick his wounds all over again.

CHAPTER 3

WELL, THAT hadn't gone the way Ash had expected. For weeks he'd managed to avoid Brighton, and when he finally met him, all he'd gotten was yelled at to show for it. He didn't understand any of Brighton's reaction. Why in the hell was he so angry? Ash was the one who had the right to be mad. He'd seen Brighton with another man and a kid. Brighton was the one who'd moved on.

Ash climbed into his truck and headed back to his aunt's. At least there things made sense and people weren't yelling at him. He drove as fast as he dared, turned into the drive, and went right inside.

"What's the rush? Did you see a ghost?" Aunt Petey asked without pausing her knitting.

Ash stopped and flopped into the chair in the living room, his leg killing him. "In a way. I bumped into Brighton, and he yelled at me. He said he thought I was dead, and…." He rubbed the back of his neck nervously.

"We all thought you were dead. The government told us that everyone was lost, and it wasn't until you returned that they said anything different." She set her needles to the side and narrowed her eyes at him. "Are you telling me you never saw him when you first got home?" She tsked and shook her head. "That boy has had a thing for you since you were kids."

"Well, he doesn't have anything for me anymore. He has a partner and a kid, and they looked pretty happy when I saw them while we were at the diner the day I brought you home." He groaned and rubbed his sore knee. It had been feeling better, but now it ached something fierce.

"You haven't talked to him? You saw him once and developed this whole narrative in your mind about what happened. He's been through a lot. I know his sister, Allison, passed away, and I believe the little girl you saw was hers."

"I didn't know. About Allison, that is." A wave of nostalgia passed over him and filled him with fond memories of Brighton and Allison arguing as children. He frowned. "But I tried to talk to him and he screamed at me." Damn, he sounded like a child.

Aunt Petey glared at him. "You had people shooting at you and you survived months in hell, but you let an outburst stop you?" She shook her head and sighed. "Sometimes men are so danged stupid." She picked up her knitting again but let it fall to her lap. "Let me ask you something. If you could have anything as far as Brighton is concerned, what would it be?"

"Oh, I don't know. Maybe for him not to have a husband, and then I could tell him what happened and we could maybe start over and try to build a life." Ash huffed loudly. "I made it through that goddamned hellhole and didn't break because I held on to him so tight that I could feel him, and then when I came back, he was kissing someone else. I don't need a block to fall on me to know what was going on. He has his own life now and doesn't need me." He hit the arm of the chair as anger and hurt mixed with confusion, and months of pent-up desire and longing washed over him. His emotions were so out of control, he couldn't sit still no matter how much his leg hurt. Ash levered himself up to hobble through the house, heading outside and into the backyard. His doctors had told him he needed to channel his aggression when it got to be too much for him, and damn it all, he could dig a channel a hundred feet deep across the damn backyard with the way he was feeling.

"Sit down and get off that leg," Aunt Petey snapped at him. He hadn't heard that tone since the time he and Brighton had used her laundry line and one of her bedsheets to make a sail.

He sat in one of the lawn chairs. "Yes, ma'am."

"I'm going back inside, and when you can think clearly and stop acting like an ass, you come in to see me and we'll talk." She left, the back door closing with a lot more force than necessary.

Ash sat there breathing deeply, doing every one of the exercises the doctors had given him to try to control the conflicting emotions that roiled in his head like a whirlpool. Finally, once he could think straight, he got back to his feet and went inside. He found Aunt Petey sitting in the same spot she had been, knitting as though nothing had happened.

"Are you ready to talk quietly?"

"Yes." Ash sat back down. "I just don't think there's anything—"

"Then let me do the talking first and you do the listening." She lowered her knitting to her lap. "You and Brighton have been friends since you were twelve years old, and you two loved each other more than life itself. Now, put yourself in his shoes and tell me what he's thinking right now."

Son of a bitch. Aunt Petey always had a way of boiling things down until they were so damn obvious and simple to understand, especially this emotional shit. "He's angry."

"Come on. You can do better than that!" she snapped sharply. "He thought you were dead and now he knows you aren't, but you never came back for him. In his mind, you left him. If your uncle had done what you did, I think I'd have done more than yell at him. I'd have kicked him in the nuts and laughed as he rolled around on the ground."

"But I saw him kissing someone else. He's moved on. It's better this way." Ash sighed. Why didn't anyone see that?

"Better for who? You?" She leaned forward. "What if what you think is all wrong?" She raised her knitting and moved her fingers once again, the needles clicking softly.

He waited, watching her, but she seemed to have said her piece, and damned if she hadn't turned his world upside down.

Was it possible that he had everything wrong?

"Fuck...," Ash groaned under his breath.

43

"Don't use that language in this house," Aunt Petey said, not stopping her knitting for a second.

"You can swear like a sailor. I've heard you."

She smiled. "But it's my house and I'm an old lady. There are privileges that come with age." Her needles clicked faster. "So, are you going to fucking sit there all day or go find out what's really going on?" She tilted her head to one side, glaring at him.

"I don't know where to find him," Ash said, which sounded dumb even to his own ears.

"I bet Rose does," Aunt Petey offered.

Ash sat still, thinking, running scenarios through his head, and they all seemed to end badly. But one thing was perfectly clear—no matter how they ended, he was no worse off than he was now. And in the one that had a positive outlook, the ending was what he'd dreamed about for months while he was a prisoner. He gave that scenario a near zero chance of working out, but he had to know. Ash got to his feet and hobbled to the door, Aunt Petey continuing her knitting. When he turned, he saw her smiling.

Ash left the house and returned to his truck to head back toward town and hopefully some of the answers that he needed almost as badly as he needed to breathe.

AN HOUR later, after he'd sweet-talked Rose as best he could, Ashton stood on the sidewalk outside the door to the apartment above the small shoe repair shop on Main Street. He looked up at the deep green façade and then down at his feet. Shit, he hadn't been this nervous about anything since he'd been a prisoner of the Taliban, in a cell in Pakistan.

"Man up," he told himself and knocked on the door. He wasn't sure if the stairs went directly to the apartment or if there was another door, and he didn't want to impose on whoever was inside. Ash waited until he heard footsteps on the stairs and held

44

his breath as the door opened. He'd hoped to see Brighton, but it was the other man, the one he'd seen kiss Brighton.

"Can I help you?" he asked, standing in the doorway.

Ash straightened up as best he could. "I'd like to talk to Brighton, please."

"He's upstairs, and I don't think he wants to see anyone. Can you come back later?" The guy seemed nice enough, but Ash hated him on sight.

"I'm Ash, and I really need to see Brighton." He put his hand on the door, prepared to push his way inside. "There are things I really need to talk to him about."

"I'm Raymond, his cousin, and I don't think he has anything to say to you. Now, I suggest—" He began closing the door.

"Wait!" Ash snapped. "You're his cousin? Not his partner?" He wanted to get down on his knees and thank God for whatever good fortune was smiling down on him. "But I thought—"

"What are you doing here, Ash?" Brighton said from behind Raymond. "We don't have anything to say to each other."

"Yes, we do! I came back for you. I did! I came back for you and saw you with him and thought you'd moved on." Ash reached past Raymond for Brighton. "I came back for you." In his dreams, when he reached out for Brighton, he was always out of reach, but Brighton stepped closer, and Ash touched his arm, fumbled for his shoulder, and held on. "I came back for you...." It was all he seemed to be able to say.

"When?" Brighton breathed.

"A year ago, once I got out of the hospital. I saw you and him cross the street." Ash pointed toward Raymond, who was retreating up the stairs. "He kissed you, and I thought you'd moved on and I didn't want to saddle you with what I've become. So I left." Ash hadn't cried over anything in years, not since the day he left Brighton for that last damned mission, but tears filled his eyes now.

"Why didn't you come to me?" Brighton stepped outside, and Ash wrapped him in his arms. "You should have talked to me. I thought you were dead." Brighton trembled in his arms. "Don't think this means I forgive you for not finding me." He held him tighter. "A year ago… you came here a year ago? That's when you saw me?"

"Yes." Ash leaned down, inhaling Brighton's clean scent, remembering the first time he'd gotten to do that. Brighton smelled just the same: sunshine and rain, mixed with apples. Ash knew it sounded dumb, but it was what he smelled. He had never been so happy to have been wrong in his life.

Brighton loosened his grip and stepped back. "You stayed away a whole year without talking to me?"

Ash nodded. "I didn't know you thought I was dead. I was taken prisoner. The government—"

"They told us nothing. We all assumed you were dead after not hearing anything for months. The whole town did." Brighton looked both ways and took Ash by the hand. "Come on inside. We can talk."

Ash wasn't sure if that was a victory or not. There were so many things he needed to try to explain, and he had a million questions himself. Brighton climbed the stairs, and Ash followed, careful of his knee. By the time he made it to the top, he wished he'd brought some painkillers with him. Brighton opened the door at the top of the stairs and motioned him into the apartment.

A little girl slept under a light blanket on the sofa.

"Is that your sister's daughter?"

"You know about Violet?" Brighton asked.

"Aunt Petey told me you were raising her. She's the one who told me to pull my head out of my a… er, butt and come to see you." Ash sighed, and Brighton motioned him to a chair at the small kitchen table. Ash followed Brighton with his gaze. He was older and much more harried than the man with the quick smile and light that shone in his eyes that Ash had left. And Ash knew a lot of the changes were his fault.

46

"What happened to you?" Brighton brought him a glass of tea and sat across from him.

"Do you need me here with you?" Raymond asked, crossing his arms over his chest, glaring at Ash.

"No. I'm fine." Brighton smiled, and for a second, he was just as Ash remembered. He wanted to reach out and take Brighton's hand, but he wasn't sure if he had the right. "Will you check on Violet? She should probably wake up and have something to drink."

"Of course." Raymond flashed Ash one more glare and turned away, heading over to the sofa.

Brighton sat there, staring for a few minutes. "I don't know where to begin. I really thought you were dead. I've been mourning and wishing for you for a year and a half... and you were alive and out there... and I didn't know it."

"Yes. I was alive, but not living.... I haven't been living... really living... since I left." Ash wrapped his hands around the cool glass.

"I don't know what to ask you first," Brighton said quietly.

"How about I try to explain what happened? That's why I came here." Ash tapped the glass with his fingers, thinking. "There are things I can't tell you and many things I won't tell you." That was the best way he could put it.

"Don't you think I can handle it?" Brighton asked in a soft voice filled with skepticism. "I haven't had things all that easy."

"It isn't about you understanding. It's about me not wanting you to be touched by it. I'll explain as best I can." Ash took a deep breath. "You know I was supposed to serve out my last few weeks officially at Carlisle Barracks, but I was using up the last of my leave and then I was supposed to be discharged. They needed someone with my tactical skills, and my Ranger unit was being sent overseas for what was supposed to be a quick in-and-out. Well, things went to hell fast once we were on the ground, and I was captured." There was no need to go into

47

any further detail as far as he was concerned. The barest facts were all that was required. He pushed on. "My mission was classified—still is. But it was really bad, and the Army hushed it all up. I was taken prisoner." He knew what was coming next and held up his hand. "Don't ask me about it, please. I can't talk about it with you... or anyone." He drank some tea to wet his now-dry throat.

"Is that the reason you're limping?" Brighton asked, and Ash nodded. His knee seemed to know they were talking about it and began aching more forcefully. "Do you need anything?"

"Ibuprofen if you have it," he answered, and Brighton left the table and returned with a couple of pills that he handed to Ash. "Thanks."

"How long were you held?" He sat down slowly.

Ash popped the pills into his mouth and downed them with the tea. "About four months, though it was hard for me to keep track at the time. They used to let me outside sometimes, and I did my best to try to leave clues that could be caught from the air. One of my messages got through, and intelligence realized someone was alive and mounted a rescue. After that, I was flown to a base hospital, where they put what was left of me back together. They also debriefed me about everything they could think of." His hand shook, and he gripped the glass a little tighter to try to cover it up. "I was really broken then. I had doctors and headshrinkers talking to me all the time. They finally let me out a year ago, and I came back here to see you."

"Why didn't you call me when you were in the hospital?" Brighton asked. "I would have come to see you."

"I couldn't. They didn't want the enemy to know where I was or how I'd been rescued. It was all kept secret, so they even kept me out of sight in the military hospital. I finally got permission to call Aunt Petey, but she had to swear to keep the information secret, and the FBI checked her out before I could call her to let her know I was doing okay. Once they let me out, I came back here to look for you, and I saw you with Raymond. I tried to call, but your number was out of service." Ash leaned forward. "I saw him kiss you."

"He's my cousin. Raymond might have kissed me, but it wasn't the way you and I used to kiss." Brighton closed his eyes a second. "After you didn't come back, I fell apart. I'd been missing you for months, with no word, and then you were given up for dead and… I needed help, and Raymond needed a place to stay after things got really weird with his parents."

Raymond came over, carrying Violet, her head resting on his shoulder. "He was a real mess."

"Thanks…," Brighton groused.

"You were. And then, when he got his feet under him again, things changed again, and he took over taking care of the princess here."

Brighton looked up at her, smiling. "This is Violet."

"I'm hungry, Uncle Brighton." She squirmed, and Raymond carefully passed her onto Brighton's lap.

"I'll make you some toast, and we'll see how your tummy is." Raymond went to the kitchen.

"So you saw us and thought Raymond and I were together?" Brighton asked.

"Yeah. I was pretty low and figuring a whole lot of things out." It was hard to explain that, after months of captivity, he wasn't sure of anything any longer. They'd played enough games with his mind and body that Ash had questioned everything, including who he was. "I saw you and figured you were better off with him than with a guy so messed up, he could barely walk. My head was a disaster." He looked down at the table. "It still is."

Brighton reached across the table to take his hand, and Ash sighed, closing his eyes to focus his entire attention on the gentle touch. "How did you get through all that?"

Ash slowly got to his feet and walked around the table. "I should be going. You have more important things to deal with than me talking about what's past. I'm staying with Aunt Petey. I brought her back from the nursing home and am helping take care of her." He bent down to the little girl, who stared at him with the biggest blue eyes, which were almost as pretty as her uncle's. "You're very pretty," Ash told her. "I knew your uncle when he was a boy."

Violet nodded and looked up at Brighton, then back at him. "Do you kiss boys like Uncle Brighton does?" She smiled up through her lashes.

"Violet!"

"Uncle Brighton, you said you kiss the ones you care about. He was holding your hand. If you care about him, do you kiss him?"

Ash shook his head slightly. That was one little girl who didn't miss much.

"I used to kiss your Uncle Brighton, but that was a while ago and I think I lost that right." Ash patted Brighton on the shoulder and hobbled to the door, but stopped with his hand on the knob. "To answer your question, I got through it all because I held on to you and every memory I had of you. They could take everything they wanted, but they weren't going to take that away." He turned, opened the door, and left the apartment, closing the door behind him.

Ash reached the bottom of the stairs and sighed. At least he'd been able to say what he needed to. He didn't know if Brighton understood or if he would give him a chance, but at least he'd cleared the air. Why would Brighton want him anyway? He wasn't the same man he'd been before he left. Hell, he couldn't walk right, and there was the possibility that he never would, even after all the surgeries and therapy. Plus, Ash was still figuring out who he really was now.

He limped to his truck and got inside, heaving a sigh of relief as the ache receded. He needed to get home, put a heating pad on his knee, and try to rest it.

"How DID it go?" Aunt Petey asked as he lowered himself into the living room chair a little while later.

50

"I guess he wasn't too mad at me. He and I talked." Ash closed his eyes and sighed. "You were right. The guy I saw him with was his cousin." He groaned. "To think I wasted an entire year, and if I'd have just gone up to him then…." He was fairly sure if he had, things would be so much different now. For one thing, it was very possible that he and Brighton would be ensconced together in a small house somewhere, with Brighton's niece. "I think I blew everything."

"No, honey. You've been through a lot, and so has he." She put her knitting in her basket and sat back. "Neither of you is the same man you were before you left. Give him some time. He knows you're back, and if you explained things right, then he knows you aren't some asshole who just left him. He needs a chance to think about what he wants." She leaned forward, catching Ash's gaze and holding it. "You need to do the same."

"I know what I want because it's what I never stopped wanting more than anything else." His entire body missed Brighton, like the loss of a limb.

"Then win him back. Show him how much he means to you." She shook her head in that way that said he was being completely stupid. "God, you men can be so muddleheaded. You like him, and you expect Brighton to see you and be overjoyed, maybe jump into your arms, and then take you to the bedroom so you can hump each other's brains out. Afterward you'd profess your undying love and that would be it. Happily ever after, the end." She rolled her eyes.

"What's wrong with wanting that?" Ash relaxed, and some of the ache left his leg.

"Nothing. But it doesn't come that easily. It never does. You need to work for it." She gingerly got to her feet, and Ash watched her walk toward the bathroom. He listened in case she needed any help, and once she was back, he closed his eyes and tried to rest his knee and get a little breather.

THE FOLLOWING morning, at lunchtime, Ash walked into Hansen's drugstore. Looking around, he discovered the place hadn't changed at all. The old floor still shone, and the aging store was completely spotless and smelled of Pine-Sol and floor wax. He made his way up the aisles until he found Brighton building a display of shampoo.

"Hey."

"Hi," Brighton said with a nervous smile. "Do you need something?"

"I was wondering if you'd like to go to lunch?" Ash didn't know why he was so jittery. He and Brighton had eaten lunch together many hundreds, maybe thousands of times, but he couldn't stop the butterflies in his belly.

"My break is in ten minutes. I can meet you at the Apple Diner if you like." Brighton's lips curled upward, and there was a touch of the light in his eyes that Ash remembered so well.

"I have to pick up a few things for Aunt Petey. I can take care of that and walk you over." Ash wasn't going to give up a second of time with Brighton if he could help it. He pulled out the list Aunt Petey had given him and began shopping.

By the time he had the things Aunt Petey needed, including creams and ointments that Ash never thought he'd have to buy, he stood, holding the plastic bag, as Brighton walked his way. Ash smiled, *really* smiled as Brighton sent a warmth through him. Brighton wore normal blue jeans with a gray polo shirt, the Hansen's logo embroidered on it, but the sight was as beautiful and as welcome as anything he could remember.

"Are you ready?"

"Yes. I only have an hour," Brighton said.

Ash pushed open the front door and held it for Brighton. "I know. I thought I remembered your schedule and was hoping it hadn't changed." He paused long enough to put the bag in his truck as they passed.

"Does your knee hurt a lot?" Brighton smiled and took his arm, and Ash leaned on him a little.

"Yeah. They did a number on it." He didn't want to go into detail. "I was lucky, though. The doctors said that they could save it, and they have repaired most of the damage, a little bit at a time. It's healing now, and in a few weeks, they'll take the brace off and I should be good to go. I try to stay off it as much as I can, but some people have stairs that lead halfway to Everest...."

Brighton nudged his side. "I'm happy you came yesterday." They waited at the corner and crossed the street when it was safe. "And I'm sorry I yelled at you. I was really mad because I thought you didn't care and that you'd... left me."

"No." Ash could see now that it had all been so stupid. "I thought you'd moved on."

"I've been trying, or I had been, sort of. Raymond kept telling me that I needed to go out and date, but it didn't feel right. Not like it was cheating, but I didn't want anyone else. Then Allie got cancer, and I spent a lot of time with her and Violet. We hoped she'd pull through, and then we prayed for a miracle, but it never came." Brighton pulled open the door to the diner, and they walked inside the crowded restaurant. The Apple Diner was an institution at lunch, and Rose hurried over and led them to the only empty spot in the place. She cleared off the dishes and wiped the table as they sat.

"I'll have a Coke and a... Dr Pepper?" He caught Brighton's gaze, and Brighton nodded.

"I'll be back as soon as I can." As Rose hurried away, Ash wondered how someone her age could keep up the pace she did. Maybe the old adage of "use it or lose it" was true.

"I'm sorry about Allie. Your sister was an amazing woman." She used to play with them sometimes, but since she was about four years older than them, their interests didn't really line up most of the time. "What about your parents?"

"They're good. I'm closer to Mom than to Dad."

"Why didn't they take Violet?" Ash asked, pausing to thank Rose as she set down the glasses.

"Do you know what you want?" Rose asked, her pad out and pen ready.

53

"I'm going to have a BLT on white toast with the fries, and I need a burger to go for Aunt Petey." Ash smiled. "I've been worried about her eating, but she loves your burgers."

"Then I'll make what she likes and have it for you when you leave." Rose turned to Brighton, who ordered a Reuben sandwich. Ash knew exactly what Brighton wanted before he'd said a word, old memories coming forward once again. "Is that all?"

"Thank you," Ash told her, and Rose was off to the kitchen, taking drink refill orders as she went.

"To answer your question, Allie requested that I take her. I don't think she ever fully forgave my parents for the way they acted when I came out, and she didn't want Violet exposed to their attitudes. She's five and will start kindergarten in the fall. Now she goes to a combination of preschool and day care." Brighton leaned over the table, his eyes full of sadness. "She gave me something to live for."

"I know how you feel." Ash gulped his drink, trying not to let the overwhelming sadness and despair overflow.

"I know you do," Brighton whispered, and to Ash's shock, he took his hand right there in the diner. "I see…." Brighton held his gaze, and Ash wanted to look away but didn't dare. Instead, he tried to keep his gaze blank, but hiding things from Brighton was hard. "I see what you've been through." Brighton blinked and backed away. "So much pain," he said quietly, squeezing Ash's hand.

Ash couldn't move. He felt so damned exposed, even more so than when he'd been hypnotized by one of his doctors. Afterward he'd wondered what he'd said and refused to allow the process ever again. The doctor had told him that he would remember everything, but Ash still wondered. The thing was, he wanted to look away and shut off whatever was going on between them, but he couldn't. Brighton could always look into his soul. It was a pathway that Ash had opened to him so long ago, and his mind knew it and forgot how to hide things from him.

Brighton gasped and blinked. "I won't ask you to tell me what those bastards did to you. I know you won't."

Ash swallowed and nodded. Not unless Brighton dragged it out of him. "You don't need to have that darkness as part of your life. No one does."

"But you carry it with you." Ash half expected Brighton to pull away, but he squeezed his hand again. "I'm sorry you had to go through all that... alone."

The last word, breathed like a prayer, sent a chill through Ash, and his hand shook. He could never tell Brighton just how alone he'd been. Cut off from everything and everyone, the only information he'd received was from his captors. Thankfully, at least a few times, someone in the camp had a radio and liked Western music, so he heard brief snippets of news and was able to reorient himself to the time and date. That alone had been a blessing. Otherwise, they had fed him what they wanted him to know to see how he'd react.

"Let's talk about something much more fun," Ash suggested. "Do you still go swimming?" He didn't have to force a smile as an image of Brighton in his red board shorts came to mind. Of course, his mind also conjured up later, when he and Brighton were alone and Ash got to slide those boardies over Brighton's hips and down his legs.

Brighton smiled. "I know what you're thinking." He glanced away, grinning. "You always had a thing for going swimming and then having some fun afterward." Dang, the smirk on Brighton's face was naughty. Not that Brighton wasn't just as randy as Ash had been. "Yes, I like swimming. But there aren't a lot of places to go around here. I'm hoping this summer that I can find somewhere for Violet to learn to swim."

Ash looked up as Rose brought their plates. "Thank you."

"You're welcome, sweetheart. Here's your check, and I added the food for your aunt. It will be out in ten minutes or so."

"Perfect. Aunt Petey will be happy."

"Do you want me to send some tea along with it?" Rose turned, not waiting for an answer, and Ash hoped to hell he didn't get stopped with that stuff on the way home.

55

"How is your aunt? I've been meaning to come see her...."

"She's doing better now that she's home. She knits up a storm, and I swear she watches more daytime television than anyone has a right to. I got a big-screen TV so I could watch the games, but I never even get to watch anything because she has her stories on and I can never find the remote. I think she hides it in her knitting bag." Not that he was upset. If it made Aunt Petey happy, he was all for it. She and his uncle had given him more than he could ever repay.

"Do you watch a lot of sports?"

Ash shook his head. "But it would be nice to watch something other than *The Golden Girls*. I swear that show is on twenty-four hours a day." He took a bite of his sandwich and groaned. There was nothing better than a BLT with plenty of mayo.

Brighton laughed and bit into his Rueben, the toasted bread crunching as he did so. "What have you done since you got out of the hospital that first time?"

"They let me out, and I came here. But I still had months of therapy, and I've had three surgeries. Two on my leg and one on my hand." Ash slipped that hand under the table, knowing Brighton would look at it. "They broke my fingers, and I set them as best I could. The surgeons were able to fix it." He pulled his hand out, figuring he was being dumb, and Brighton took it and gently rubbed it as he looked it over. "There're just the scars now. I can use it pretty normally."

"Did they hurt you in other places?" Brighton swallowed, and Ash grabbed his glass, wishing there was some rum in with the soda.

"They did a lot to me. Let's leave it at that. After a while, it wasn't about what I knew or what they thought I knew. It became personal to one of the men. He thought it was some sort of battle between the two of us. He was determined to break me and get me to tell him whatever he wanted to know." Ash's leg quivered under the table, though he was pretty proud that he kept most of the anger and hatred out of his voice and off his face. "If I ever see him again, I swear I'll kill the bastard." That wasn't likely, but if he got the chance, he wasn't going to let it pass.

Ash sighed. Every topic of conversation led back to the same thing. "Anyway, after months of rehab, surgery, more rehab, and God knows what, I was released and I came to get Aunt Petey. She was doing better, so I got some friends to help me clean up the house for her. They did most of the work because I can't stand for very long."

"I always loved that house. We used to go in the attic and pretend it was a ship and we were sailing across the seas." Brighton smiled. "There are all those cubbyholes and nooks that we used to explore." He finished his sandwich and checked his watch. "Oh God. I've got ten minutes and I have to be back."

"It's all right. Finish eating, and I'll take care of the check. You just go when you need to." Ash smiled, happy to be with Brighton again. "Why don't you and Violet come over? Aunt Petey would love to see you again, and I'm sure she'd love to meet Violet. Is she feeling better?"

"Yes. She was excited to go back to school and see her friends today. I think it was probably something she ate or a touch of the flu. Her temperature was back to normal when we put her to bed, and she was fine this morning. I'd have probably kept her home, but it's hard when both Raymond and I need to work."

"Just call. Aunt Petey would love to have someone around that she could spoil. So much of the time, she's at home with the television. Some of her friends come over, but she'd adore spending time with your little girl."

Brighton ate the last of his fries and finished his Dr Pepper with a slurp. "If you're sure...."

"Of course. Aunt Petey keeps wanting to cook, and every time she does, we have enough food for a week. So please come and save me before the pot roast takes over everything." Ash smiled and stood as Brighton did. "I'll see you later." He wasn't sure what to do, but he didn't want Brighton to leave without knowing how he felt. Rose would tolerate a lot of things, but he didn't think kissing in front of half the town was a good idea.

"Definitely. And thanks for lunch." Brighton gave a little wave and hurried out of the restaurant and across the street.

"Rose, you allow fags in here?"

Ash turned around and followed the voice to one of the men sitting at the counter.

"You shut your mouth, Delbert. I allow people in here who have manners and know how to behave. Since you don't, I suggest you get your ass up off that stool and out the door." Rose pulled away his cup and set it in the dish bin.

"You're kicking me out?" Delbert didn't move.

"I sure am. You talk about others as though you're some sort of saint, when I know you're carrying on with some slut behind your wife's back. So get out and don't show your smelly, sorry butt in here again." She turned away, and two of the other patrons stood, ready, it seemed, to show him the door.

Delbert shot daggers at Ash, but he turned and left the diner, slamming the door in a fit. Rose flipped the guy the bird, and half the patrons laughed and then returned to their conversations.

"Thanks," Ash told her as he paid the check and took the burger for Aunt Petey.

"Some people think we're still in the dark ages and they can spout their opinions anywhere they want." Rose spoke loud enough that everyone could hear. "He can be a jackass if he wants, just not under my roof. And when his wife finds out what the slack-jawed yokel has been up to, I'd say he's not going to have much of a roof of any kind over his head." She smiled and handed him the to-go cup of iced tea. "Drive safely, now."

"I still appreciate it."

"Honey. You served this country the same as anyone else, and you came back a lot worse for wear because of it. You're a hero—

don't let anyone ever tell you different." She patted his shoulder and left to take another order.

Ash picked up the bag and cup and left the diner, wishing to hell he felt like a hero.

He got to his truck, put the cup in the holder and the bag on the seat, and headed home. One thing he was going to need to do was get a damn job. He had pay saved up, and he'd gotten a huge bonus for his wounds and for hazardous duty. Mostly it was money he'd been paid on the stipulation that he keep his mouth shut about what happened and how fucked-up it had all been. It was the American way, after all. Money talked and bullshit walked.

"Aunt Petey?" Ash called as he came into the house.

"Ash, is that you?" she asked, sounding frail.

He set down the bag and cup and hurried toward her voice. He found her in the kitchen, sitting on the floor, the chair a bit away. "What happened? Are you all right?" He wondered if he should help her up or call an ambulance.

"I slipped and fell. I was trying to sit down, and the chair got away. I ended up down here, with the chair way over there." She reached for his hand, and he gave it. "I'm fine. Nothing hurt but my pride."

He helped her to her feet and got her seated at the table. Then he grabbed a plate and put her burger on it. "Rose sent you some tea as well. But you better have that once you're in your chair."

Aunt Petey shook her head and snorted. "I've been having Rose's special tea since she and I were twenty and decided we wanted to see what all the whoopee was about. We liked it. For a long time, we didn't make it because we were 'responsible.'" She made air quotes with her fingers. "But when we got older and the aches and pains caught up with us, she started making it again, and it helps." She smiled and reached for the cup. She sipped, then unwrapped the burger and dug in like she hadn't eaten in three days. "How was lunch?"

"Nice. We talked, and he held my hand." Ash pulled out a chair and sat next to her.

59

"That's so… eighth grade." She laughed. No one could tease him the way Aunt Petey could.

"I didn't think Rose would appreciate me kissing Brighton within an inch of his life right there in the diner. Although she did kick some guy out for making a comment."

"If you and Brighton kissed in the diner, she'd probably watch. That Rose is one horndog. She married Wilbur and they've been happy, but I swear if she hadn't, that woman would have humped the entire male population of Adams County." She hooted. "So yeah. Rose probably would have wolf-whistled and yelled encouragement."

"Okay." He wasn't sure he was ready for that either. "Thanks for sharing. You know, you never would have told me those kind of things when I was younger."

Aunt Petey shrugged. "You're twenty-six now—you can handle it." She turned to him, grinning. "What? You think your generation invented sex and all the other good stuff? Hell no. My generation did." She threw her head back, laughing. "At least that's what my mother told me once. So get over yourself and let go of some of this shit." She passed him the Styrofoam cup of tea. "Maybe you need this more than I do."

Ash shook his head, pushing it back. "I…. For a while there, I did a lot worse than special tea. I was trying to forget and make everything go away. So I don't want to take anything I don't have to." He stood. "Eat your lunch. I'm going into the living room to put my leg up. Just leave the dishes when you're done, and I'll take care of them later." Ash went into the other room, then poked his head back in. "Oh, and before you argue, I'm getting you a cell phone. I'll program the numbers, and that way if you fall, you'll have a way to contact help."

"Fine. I just won't have one of those stupid 'I've fallen and I can't get up' buttons. I'm not that old, and I will not be that helpless."

Ash didn't point out that's exactly what had just happened. There was nothing wrong with her temper. That was for sure.

"I'll get you one as soon as I can. In the meantime, wear the good shoes. Those slippers are slick." They were probably the reason she'd fallen in the first place. "You don't want to hurt yourself and end up back in the home." And Ash didn't want her back there either. "So please be careful."

Ash went to sit in his chair and put his leg up, looking forward to tomorrow.

CHAPTER 4

"How did it go with Ethan?" Brighton asked after Violet was in bed that night. He'd waited up for Raymond because he hadn't seen him all day.

"Really nice. He's an interesting guy and knows all kinds of famous people." Raymond sat down gently, and Brighton knew exactly why.

"Do you really like him, or are you just interested in who he is and the people he knows?" Brighton asked, smirking. "You said yourself that he's only here for a few weeks and then he's supposed to go back to LA."

"I really like him, and we don't spend all our time talking about the people he knows. Ethan's really smart and he's seen the world, at least a lot more of it than I have." Raymond seemed really excited, and the lilt in his voice was nice to hear, but Brighton was really afraid that Raymond was setting himself up for a fall. "He's had the same kind of luck with guys that I have."

Brighton raised his eyebrows. "What? He picks losers too?" He couldn't help getting in the dig, just a little. Raymond had terrible taste in men. He went for big guys with more muscles than brains, then wondered why they weren't interesting and got bored with them.

"Ha-ha…." Raymond sat back. "He says that most guys out there always have one eye on the door. They're with you and watching in case someone better comes along."

"And you're the someone better?" Brighton regretted the words as soon as they crossed his lips. "I don't mean that to sound bitchy." He kept his voice low, not wanting to wake Violet. "I just don't want you to get hurt. This Ethan comes in from LA for a few weeks of fun and then he goes home, back to his life… and you're left here with a broken heart." Brighton's voice broke. "I know how that feels."

Raymond nodded. "How are you doing now that Ash is back?"

Brighton's lips turned upward. "He came to the store and took me to lunch." He got up, poured a couple glasses of tea from the refrigerator, and brought them back, handing one to Raymond. "He's the same and yet he's different."

"How so?"

"I still see the man I love in him. But there's another part, something he's keeping hidden and closed off. Ash doesn't want to talk about what happened to him, but he did tell me some things." He sipped the tea and set the glass on a coaster on the old wood coffee table. "It worries me."

"Okay." Raymond patted his knee. "Does it worry you enough to stop seeing him? To turn away?"

Brighton shook his head. "Ash is back and he's alive."

Raymond chuckled at his exuberance. "This is what you've hoped for."

"Yes, and my heart is beating so fast that I can hear it constantly. When we said goodbye, I wanted to kiss him. I mean, I wanted to push him down on the table and kiss the life out of him. I wanted to hold him and never let him out of my sight again." He could barely keep still, he was so happy. "It seems so long since I did, I don't know if I can remember what it's like." He felt his cheeks heat as he thought of how Ash tasted—earthy, rich, with a touch of saltiness that sent him into orbit. He needed to know if Ash was still the same, if his hands would feel the same, and if Ash's heart would touch his the way it had before.

"Why didn't you? I'm sure Rose would have cheered you on."

Brighton chuckled. "No reason other than we were in public. I wanted to." Ash was the sun drawing his planet into orbit. Or maybe Brighton was a comet being pulled ever closer and closer to Ash's sun, just hoping he didn't burn up. "But then I thought of Violet and knew I had to take things slowly. I can't rush into something that could hurt her."

"But you deserve to be happy," Raymond said softly.

"So do you. Just, please, be careful." Brighton took Raymond's hand. "Maybe you could arrange for me to meet Ethan."

"I think I'd like that, and maybe I can meet Ash. Officially."

"Then I'll try to set something up for the four of us. My mother would be happy to watch Violet and spend more time with her." He sat back and was taking another sip from his glass when his phone dinged. He picked it up, smiled, and showed the message to Raymond.

"That's so very nice. Go ahead and call him if you want." Raymond turned on the television, keeping the volume low, while Brighton went into his bedroom and closed the door.

"Thank you for your message. But how did you get my number?"

"I looked it up," Ash said. "The internet is a wonderful thing, and now you have mine." He seemed so pleased. "I spoke with my aunt, and she'd love to have you and Violet over for dinner. She asked about Friday, but if that's too soon...."

"No. I work during the day, so that will work." He hesitated. "I'm sorry...."

"Let me guess—your cousin?" Ash could always read him like a book. "Bring him as well. Aunt Petey always cooks for an army, so bring as many friends as you'd like."

"Are you sure?"

"Yes. If Raymond is seeing someone.... Aunt Petey will love meeting new people."

Brighton sighed, grateful for Ash's generosity. "Raymond is seeing a guy from LA, and I'm worried he's just stringing Raymond along while he's here. Maybe you can help sniff him out and see what he's up to."

"I'd be glad to." Ash chuckled. "I had a great lunch today. The only thing was that it wasn't long enough."

"I felt the same way. Just like before, I could have stayed and talked for hours. Maybe we can have lunch again tomorrow?"

"I'd like that. At the same time? I can meet you at the store."

"I'll see you then, and I'll tell Raymond about Friday." He wanted to say something about how he felt, but everything was so muddled, he was afraid to. Instead, he kept quiet and got ready to hang up.

"Brighton…," Ash said, and Brighton's thumb paused over the End button. "I want you to know, I never stopped loving you. Not when I was being held, and even after I thought you were with someone else. I missed you every day, and I still miss you when you're not here." Ash paused, and the phone shook in Brighton's hand.

"I missed you too," he managed to croak out around the lump in his throat, then ended the call.

Brighton sat on the edge of his bed for a while, just thinking and smiling to himself. He wanted to believe Ash, but the part about Ash staying away and not even talking to him didn't sit well, and he needed a chance to work through that. Ash was putting in some effort and not taking for granted that Brighton would just come running back to him; that was nice.

"Brighton," Raymond said through the cracked-open door. "Violet was stirring. I turned off the television, and she seems to have quieted again."

"Okay." Brighton motioned for Raymond to come inside. "Ash invited us to his aunt's for dinner on Friday, and he said you could bring a guest if you wanted."

Raymond cocked his eyebrows. "So, you figured I could bring Ethan, and the two of you could check him out."

"Yup." Brighton grinned. "Ash will help me find out his intentions." He stood, puffing out his chest. "Make sure he's good enough for our little Raymond." It took him two seconds before he dissolved into giggles that he managed to stifle before he woke Violet. "Aunt Petey is a great cook, and Ash was saying that she cooks big. You'll love the place, and so will Violet." He sat back, thinking. "I wonder if Ash rebuilt the treehouse. The swing and stuff probably are."

"Okay. I'll ask Ethan if he wants to join us." Raymond rolled his eyes.

"Don't worry, I'll be nice. I don't want you getting hurt."

"I could say the same thing to you," Raymond retorted.

Brighton groaned. "We're like a couple of old hens looking out for each other." Maybe that wasn't so bad. "It's getting late and I need to be at the store early. A big shipment is coming in."

"Do you need me to see Violet off to school?"

"If you could, that would be awesome." He could get in a little earlier to start, and hopefully the bulk of the stock to be shelved could be done before the store opened. "It would be a huge help."

"No problem. I'll see you in the morning."

"Thanks. Good night."

Raymond left the door open and went to his room while Brighton checked on Violet, who was sleeping soundly, tucked under her covers. He was so blessed.

"I wish you were here to see her, Allie. She's so much like you." Brighton went back into his room and got ready for bed.

"ARE YOU ready to go to Ash's house? His aunt is making us dinner," Brighton said to Violet as soon as he picked her up at day care.

"Does she have kids I can play with?"

"No. But there's a swing in the backyard, and you can bring some of your toys." He got her buttoned up and took her hand to walk home. It was a gorgeous spring day, with the sweet floral scent filling the calm air. "Will that be okay?"

She thought a minute, bringing her fingers to her mouth. "Yes."

Brighton lifted her into his arms to swing her around, to Violet's delight. He set her down and continued the walk home as his phone rang. "Hey, Raymond."

66

"Ethan just called. He says he can't come tonight. His boss's mother's plans fell through, and she's sitting at the hotel. Ethan doesn't want to leave her alone."

"Let me call Ash. From what he said, I don't think it will be a problem." Brighton hung up and dialed Ash, who seemed delighted.

"Of course, tell him to bring her. The more, the merrier." Ash sounded really excited, and Brighton called Raymond back.

"Tell Ethan to bring whoever he needs to. Apparently Ash's aunt decided to cook an entire beef roast and there's a ton of food." He hung up, and they walked the rest of the way home.

"Uncle Raymond!" Violet cried when they reached the top of the stairs. She hugged him, then hurried to her room because she knew exactly what she wanted to wear.

Brighton wasn't convinced, but he went to change and then made sure Violet's clothes weren't blinding. Then, once they were ready, they headed down to Raymond's car for the short drive to Aunt Petey's.

"Ethan said he'd be here in half an hour," Raymond explained as he pulled into the long drive and parked behind Ash's truck.

They got out, and Violet walked with Brighton toward the house, then stopped out front to look up. "Are there ghosts in there?" she asked, pointing to the top of the tower.

"Nope. I used to play up there with Ash when we were younger. But there might be some toys still up there, and maybe if you're good, Ash will let me take you up there." The truth was that he wanted to see all those places he and Ash had explored, but that probably wasn't likely. "Let's go inside and say hello." He held her hand as they approached the door.

Ash opened it, welcoming them all inside. "Come on in." He hugged Brighton warmly, and Brighton had to stop the impulse to lean up for a kiss. He did inhale deeply, and danged if Ash's scent didn't trigger a flood of memories. He wanted to hold him for dear life.

Raymond took Violet inside. "Are they going to hug like that?" she asked.

"If they want to," Raymond told her, to Brighton's delight. "Your uncle likes Mr. Ash, and that's okay."

"Are they going to kiss?" Her tone of voice left little doubt that she was making the same face she did when Brighton asked her if she wanted a banana. Violet hated bananas.

Ash chuckled and gently tilted Brighton's head upward. "I don't think we should disappoint her. Do you?" Ash slowly leaned down and stopped a few inches from his lips. Ash held still, and Brighton didn't understand why. In the end he closed the gap, and Ash tightened his hold, kissing him harder, practically crushing their lips together. Violet's questions and Aunt Petey's laughter faded to the background as Ash deliberately pressed him against the door. "I've dreamed of this…."

Brighton hummed and kissed Ash again, reveling in the intensity of the energy that flowed between them. That was what he'd been missing this entire time. The attraction, the zing of electricity that drew them together, along with the companionship of someone who knew him as well as he knew himself. It felt as though his heart had gone from empty to filled in a matter of minutes. It was wonderful.

"I'm sorry…," Ash whispered after pulling away, cradling Brighton's chin and running a thumb over his cheek. "I stayed away because of my own stupidity and—"

"Let's let that go. You're here now." There was nothing to be done to change what had happened. They talked quietly for a while about nothing and everything, just being together. Simple companionship was wonderful. He tugged Ash down once again, kissing him as tires crunched on the drive. Ash pulled away, and Brighton followed his gaze to a huge black sedan sitting behind Raymond's car.

"Is that Ethan?" Brighton asked, turning inside to where Raymond was heading their way.

"Yes," Raymond said as he moved around them to go outside.

Ash held him tighter as Raymond dashed out toward the car and, as a man got out of the back seat, leaped into his arms. Even from there Brighton saw the smile on Ethan's face. Instantly he liked the guy who was that delighted to see his cousin. Two more men got out the other side, and one of them helped a lady out of the front seat.

"I think Ethan took your open invitation to heart." Brighton waited, then gasped as recognition washed over him. "Ash, that's Justin Hawthorne. Remember him from school? He was a few years ahead of us."

"I know," Ash said calmly as they approached.

"Hi, I'm Ethan, and this is Justin and George." They all shook hands. Brighton loved how Ethan introduced the big Hollywood movie star as though he were just another friend. "This is Justin's mother, Shirley."

"It's so nice of you to have us," Shirley said, holding a bouquet of flowers, probably for Aunt Petey.

"We're glad you can make it. Aunt Petey has cooked up a storm," Ash said with a smile that sent a shot of warmth through Brighton. He looked so happy.

"Petunia was always the consummate hostess." She patted Justin on the shoulder and stepped inside the house. Soon laugher drifted out as the two seemingly old friends got reacquainted.

"Come on in," Ash said, stepping back, still holding Brighton as the others made their way inside.

"This is an amazing house," Justin said, stopping in the impressive entranceway. "The paneled woodwork is stunning and rich." He turned to George. "You don't see things like this is LA. It's all steel and glass." Justin ran his hands over the 120-year-old, deep, rich wood, still looking around. "The details in this house are fabulous. They don't do this any longer."

"No, they don't," Ash agreed. "Would you like anything to drink? We have tea, beer, sodas, and some milk." He let his arm fall from around Brighton's waist, and Brighton felt Ash's balance leave him. He turned, holding Ash up as he leaned on the banister.

"How about if Justin and I help with the drinks while you sit down?" George offered with a smile. "We understand. Justin got hurt on a set six months ago and was laid up for a while. There's no need to push yourself."

"Thank you," Brighton said, and helped Ash into the living room and down into one of the chairs. "I'll go help while you rest your leg." He leaned in and kissed away the protest he knew was already forming. "Be right back." Brighton hurried into the kitchen, where Justin and George were trying to find the glasses.

"They're right up here," Brighton said, as at home here as he was in his own place. He was amazed that Justin, a guy who was probably used to being fawned over by everyone, seemed so normal.

"Awesome." Justin got down the glasses and started pouring tea. "This will be perfect for Mom."

"And Aunt Petey, as well as Ash and myself."

They ended up bringing in the pitcher and plenty of glasses, while Brighton got some milk for Violet. Justin carried in the tray, George the pitcher, and Brighton the milk, and then they joined the others.

"Have you decided what you're going to do now that you're home?" Shirley asked Ash as Brighton handed Violet her cup. Justin had settled on the floor with her, and they were running trucks across the living room and into the dining room, which surprised Brighton.

George stood next to him, watching Justin, while Violet giggled. "I think that's why he's so good at what he does. Justin's still a child at heart."

Brighton smiled. "It's so good to see her laughing like that." He turned, and Ash met his smile with one of his own. Brighton was contented. He hadn't thought it would ever be possible again, but he had damn near everything he ever wanted. Violet seemed happy and was settling well into their new life. Ash was back, and

Brighton's heart kept reaching out to his, and he felt the affection and care returned.

"I need to check on dinner," Aunt Petey said, standing from the sofa.

"I'll help you." Shirley joined her, and they went into the kitchen, with Shirley carrying both of their glasses.

"Violet, do you want to join us?" Aunt Petey asked, and Violet hurried after them, leaving the boys in the living room. They all took a seat, and Ash sat back, getting comfortable, some of the tension leaving his face.

"Is your knee really bothering you?" Brighton asked. "I can get you something if you need it."

"No. Just sitting is doing some good."

"Did you get in an accident?" Justin asked.

Brighton knew Ash didn't want to talk about it. "He was injured overseas and has been recovering for a while." He threaded his fingers with Ash's, perching on the arm of his chair. He patted Ash's shoulder. "He's a hero."

"The doctors say it will improve slowly and could take a couple more weeks. I need to stay off it, but things keep interfering and I end up doing too much."

As Ash grew quiet, Brighton changed the subject. "So, inquiring minds want to know." He turned to Justin. "Was that really your bare butt in that scene with Chloe, or did they use a butt double?" Brighton couldn't help himself. He snickered, and Justin thankfully smiled and laughed.

"That was really him," George answered.

"Did it bother you?" Ash asked, and Justin nodded.

"I thought about it for a while before taking the part. I mean, the camera only captured me from the back, but the crew and others got the full-on effect, if you know what I mean. Thankfully George was there to watch over things."

George nodded. "One of the crew tried to take pictures with his phone, but I saw it and he was escorted off the set." He shifted a little closer. "The last thing I wanted was pictures of him surfacing on the net, and someone would have paid a lot for them."

"Do you go with him to a lot of his filming?" Ash asked.

"Yes," Ethan answered. "I do most of the running, but sometimes I can't be two places at once, and George tends to stay close and watch over his person." He shared a glance with Raymond. "We have people who try to get on set to see him. Two weeks ago we had a group of people determined to climb the fence around the property. We had the police remove them, but sometimes it can get to be too much."

"But you love what you do," Brighton said. "That's obvious because you come across so genuine on-screen. If you didn't, you wouldn't have that feeling."

Justin leaned on George. "I do. It's the greatest job I could ever think of, but it comes with a price. Thankfully George is willing to put up with the craziness and support me." He kissed him gently, and Brighton realized he was witnessing something private. They didn't kiss in public, though there had been a few pictures that he knew of where they were holding hands. Those were rare as far as he knew. Justin narrowed his perfectly plucked eyebrows. "Don't I remember the two of you as friends? How long have you two been together?"

"Yeah. We've been friends for many years." Ash squeezed Brighton's fingers. "We're reconnecting now."

"George and I reconnected a few years ago."

Brighton leaned forward. "I saw that interview you two did on *The View*. It was wonderful and amazing to see a gay couple so happy and... secure in themselves and each other." Brighton hadn't meant to bring it up, so he turned away. Ash leaned to him and hugged him gently. "It's a long story, but I thought Ash was dead for a long time." He gripped Ash's hand.

"There's something about this town," George pronounced. "I think it has it in for people like us and rips us apart."

"Sweetheart, what happened to us was one sick bastard," Justin said, "and the town itself has been pretty supportive. Sometimes crap happens."

Violet raced in and launched herself at Brighton. "Uncle Brighton, are you talking about poo? Because that's yucky."

"No. We were talking about things that were sad." As soon as the words passed his lips, he regretted it.

"Like my mommy dying?" She leaned against him and buried her face on Brighton's chest.

Brighton held her close, but Ash stood and gently took her hand. "Sweetie, will you come with me? I lost my mommy too." He turned, leaning over, and Violet went into his arms. Brighton had to help him up, but he hobbled out of the room and into the dining room to sit with Violet. Brighton heard them whispering and Violet's sniffles and saw her hug him tight.

He bit his lip, and Raymond squeezed his shoulder. Brighton patted Raymond's hand as his heart finally let go of the last of the resentment he'd been carrying toward Ash. If he could help Violet deal with missing her mother and take the time, hurting like he was, to try to help her like that....

He turned to the others, and Justin leaned forward. "Go to them."

Brighton joined them in the dining room in time to hear Ash say, "My aunt Petey took me in and helped me, just like your uncle Brighton did for you. He loves you very much, and he will always be there for you."

"But I miss my mommy," Violet said, wiping away tears.

"Of course you do. I still miss my mommy, and she died a long time ago. It's okay to miss her. But your mommy would want you to be happy, and she'd want you to love Uncle Brighton and Uncle Raymond. Did your mommy laugh a lot?" Ash asked, and Violet nodded. "Then remember her like that, because that's what she'd want." He gathered her into his arms, hugging her gently. Brighton knew the position he was in, with one knee on the floor and the other straight out, was awkward as hell and must have been uncomfortable, but he hugged Violet while she cried. Eventually he looked up, catching Brighton's eye. "Are you going to be okay?"

Violet raised her head, nodding, leaving small wet spots on Ash's shirt.

"Do you wanna go to Uncle Brighton?" His voice was so soft, and Violet hugged Ash once again, pushing against him.

Brighton turned away. For months it seemed like she had been going through the motions in a way. Violet was a girl who liked to make people happy. Now it was time for her to be happy, and he was determined to do whatever it took, including letting someone else be there when she needed it.

Eventually Violet pushed away from Ash, and Brighton lifted her into his arms.

"Thank you," he said softly. He should have known Ash would know exactly what to say. He'd dealt with what Violet was trying to work her way through, and somehow Ash had come out on the other side. Brighton shifted Violet onto his hip as best he could and used his other hand to help Ash to his feet. "Do you want to play with your toys some more?" Brighton asked. "I bet if you ask nicely, then Mr. Justin will play with you." He smiled as Justin waved, and Violet waved back. "Go on, honey." He set her down, and she hurried over. Sure enough, Justin got on the floor, and the two of them were off once again.

"She's going to be fine."

"I hope so. She hasn't said much about her mother in a while, and I think I was stupid enough to think she was over it and moving on, but maybe the poor thing was just holding it in." There was so much more to being a parent than Brighton ever dreamed, and now he was doing it full time. "Sometimes I wonder if I'm up for this. If I'm doing the right things for her." Brighton turned away, and Ash put his hand on his shoulder. "My parents wanted to take her, but because Allie asked me to, I took her in, and now I can't see my life without her. She's…. Do you know how someone can just walk

74

into your life, and your heart, and help fill the holes that seemed gaping before?" He sniffled.

Ash used his thumb to wipe the tears from Brighton's face, and damn it all, he didn't know why the fuck he was crying. "I do. I know what it's like to feel as empty and as lonely as anyone possibly can. I questioned everything and nearly everyone in my life—the government's decisions, my friends, everything—while I was in the dark room. But the only thing I never questioned, not for a second, was you." He pulled him closer, engulfing Brighton in his strength and warmth.

"Then how... how could you walk away?" he asked, holding Ash in return.

"Because I wanted you to be happy. I wasn't going to insert myself into what looked like a happy life. I'd been gone for nine months, and I thought you had Raymond. I didn't think I had a right to come back." Ash kissed the top of his head. "I didn't think I was worth it."

Brighton shook his head slowly, inhaling the rich, manly scent that went right to his core. He ached and his pants grew tight. He wanted Ash, and if they weren't in his aunt's house with a bunch of people and Violet in the next room, he'd have rubbed himself up and down Ash like a cat wanting attention.

"You are worth it, you knucklehead." He tightened his hold, running one hand along Ash's strong back. Damn, he wanted to let his hands wander, but that whole house full of people got in the way. "You were always worth it, and you still are."

"I know that now." Ash leaned down to kiss him, and Brighton got so carried away, the hoots, whistles, and catcalls didn't even register until Ash smiled against his lips. "I think we should get back to our guests."

Brighton didn't move away. "They'll wait a few minutes." He pressed Ash back to the doorframe, stood on his toes, and kissed Ash with everything he had. The hoots started again, but they faded into the background when Ash held him once again, his fingers carding through Brighton's hair, pressing harder and humming softly.

Brighton teetered on the edge of passion and pain as the tune Ash hummed worked its way into his soul.

"I love you too," Brighton whispered softly, resting his head on Ash's shoulder. Hell, he'd never stopped. No matter what had happened between them or how far Ash had gone, knowing Ash had carried him in his heart when he left and held it close during the hours of most dire need was all he needed.

"All right, you two, that's enough of that," Raymond said as he walked over to them. "You have a room full of guys who are going to start getting restless if you keep that up." Raymond grinned wryly and turned toward the kitchen. "I think Aunt Petey needs some help."

"Okay," Ash agreed reluctantly.

"Go sit down. I'll help Aunt Petey, and maybe Violet would like to see what she can play with." Though judging by the laughter from the living room, she and Justin were having an amazing romp. Brighton hugged Ash one more time, then backed away, letting his arms slide to his sides before going through the dining room to the kitchen.

"Sweetheart, can you mash the potatoes?" Aunt Petey asked.

"Of course." He drained the potatoes and got the masher from the drawer Aunt Petey indicated, then got to work while Aunt Petey added butter, sour cream, and a little milk, as well as salt and pepper. The scent that drifted upward was homey and comforting.

"You used to love these when you were a kid. I remember you and Ash sitting at my table, eating these until you burst." She smiled, and he leaned down to kiss her cheek. Brighton had forgotten how much he loved this woman. It had been too long since he'd been to see her, and yet here she was, treating him the same as she had when he and Ash had been inseparable.

"I remember a certain lady who always made sure we had a safe place, especially when we needed it most." He put aside the potatoes for a second to hug her gently, then returned to what he was supposed to be doing.

He got the bowl, transferred the potatoes, and carried them into the dining room. He returned for the vegetables, then set out the plates and silverware while the ladies plated the roast and salad. By the time he was done, the table was ready, and Aunt Petey called everyone in to dinner. She really did cook enough for an army, and the table nearly groaned under the weight. Brighton got Violet settled in the chair next to him and fixed her a plate while the others settled. He took his seat, and Ash sat next to him, their legs bumping under the table. This felt so much like high school or maybe junior high, but he didn't care. Being happy sure beat the hell out of being lonely and miserable.

The rest of the evening was wonderful and relaxing, with plenty of food, dessert, conversation, and decaf coffee.

His mother called as they were getting up from the table. "Your dad and I just got home. Still okay for Violet to come over? I can pick her up now if you'd like."

"I'm at Aunt Petey's and we're finishing up dinner. So stop by the house in an hour. I have a bag packed for her, and you can still have her for the night." Brighton ended the call and smiled as Ash came up behind him and leaned close.

"I'll transfer the car seat and take the two of you home. Raymond and Ethan appear as if they'd like to be alone, so I can bring you back here for the night. Aunt Petey will go to sleep down here, and you and I can have the upstairs all to ourselves." Ash blew warm air over his ear, and Brighton shivered, a thrill going through him.

Justin, George, and Shirley said their good nights a few minutes later, with plenty of shared hugs.

"How long will you all be in town?" Aunt Petey asked.

"Another week, and then Justin has to be back so he can start shooting his next movie. Shirley is going back to the house in LA, and we're going to location in New Mexico." George put his arm around Justin's waist, and then after final good nights, they headed out into the night.

Ethan and Raymond said their good nights as well. Ash got his aunt settled in the living room and then took Brighton and Violet home.

His mother was waiting inside, and Violet ran to her, excited to be staying with Grandma and Grandpa. Brighton got her bag, and then the two of them left, with Violet chattering away about Uncle Brighton and Uncle Ash. Brighton grabbed a small bag of his own and threw some clothes into it.

"Do you need to get anything else?" Ash asked.

Brighton shook his head. "No." He had everything he wanted right here. He thought of taking Ash by the hand and leading him into the bedroom to take what he'd been waiting almost two years for, but Ethan and Raymond would be coming back here and he wanted to give them privacy for their reunion. Instead, he turned out the lights and locked the door on his way out.

On the street, Ash took his hand and they walked quietly— words weren't necessary—to the truck and then drove back to the house he remembered so fondly.

Aunt Petey had gone to bed, and Ash checked on her quickly, then led him up the stairs and down to the room he remembered as Ash's.

The bedroom had changed. Gone were the sports trophies and the paraphernalia of adolescence, replaced by warmth, a king-size bed, a cool, soft blue on the walls, and deep, rich wood furniture. This was the room of a man, and it wrapped around Brighton as Ash shut the door.

"I know this could be so much more romantic and all, but I need to get the brace off my leg and let it breathe." Ash sat on the edge of the bed and slowly undid the Velcro, sighing as he removed the brace and set it next to the bed. His shoes followed, and then Ash removed his shirt and pants.

That was all Brighton could take. He closed the distance between them, parted Ash's legs, and leaned down for a kiss. Ash returned it, drawing him in, and leaned back to pull them both down onto the bed.

"I know you have to be careful without the brace," Brighton whispered in Ash's ear. "So why don't you lie back and leave the driving to me." He captured Ash's lips again. "I remember what you like and what makes your eyes roll back in your head." Brighton caressed Ash's chest, then tweaked one of his nipples, teasing it with his thumb. Ash groaned as Brighton pressed closer. He had missed the heat radiating from Ash's body and the way he always felt safe in Ash's arms. Brighton moved to sit next to Ash, his gaze raking down him. Ash reached for the blanket at the foot of the bed, intent on pulling it over his knees, but Brighton placed his hand over Ash's to stop him.

"Don't."

Ash shook his head. "I don't want you to see—" He lay back down, and Brighton pushed the blanket away.

"I see you, Ash." He gently ran his hand down Ash's lower leg, rough skin bumping slightly under his fingers. Pink scars crisscrossed his leg and knee. Brighton knew some were from surgeries and others from his months in captivity. He hated them all, and yet they were part of Ash. "These are nothing to be ashamed of."

"But they're ugly."

Brighton nodded and watched as Ash's eyes widened. "They are ugly, but only because they represent the ugly things that happened to you. Nothing more." He let his hands wander upward, across Ash's thighs and to where his cock woke, sliding along his thigh before slowly reaching up toward his belly button. Brighton smiled and leaned closer, inhaling the raw musk of him. "You are never, ever ugly." His belly quivered in anger at what had been done to Ash and trembled at how much strength it must have taken for him to withstand everything. There were cuts and scars in many places, much smaller than on his legs. Most of them were ones Brighton wasn't familiar with, and he turned away for a second, his throat constricting, knowing now some of what Ash had been through. He closed his eyes and saw the pain written on Ash's face as he endured the agony in silence, gritting his teeth to keep from calling out.

Ash stroked his arm, pulling him out of his imagination. "Sweetheart…."

"I'm sorry."

Ash's excitement had deflated, and he lay there, high color on his cheeks. Brighton did his best to banish the images. He stepped off the bed, locking his gaze with Ash's as he tugged his shirt off and let it drop to the floor. His shoes and socks joined the shirt, followed by his pants and underwear. Brighton stood naked to Ash's gaze.

"We all have scars, Ash. Yours are on the outside."

"Where are yours?" Ash extended his arm, fingertips just reaching Brighton's thighs.

"Mine are here." He moved closer, took Ash's hand, and placed it on his chest. "Thankfully they're healing. It's taken some time and the return of the other half of my soul, but they're healing now. They were open for a long time, even though I didn't want to admit it." He continued closer, once again allowing his gaze to roam. Ash's chest heaved and his belly rose and fell, clenching with each breath. Brighton climbed back on the bed and straddled Ash, mindful not to put too much weight on him.

"Why would you wait so long for me?" Ash asked, his voice breaking.

Brighton leaned forward. "Because you're worth it." He held still. "Because you have the other half of my heart—you always have. You took it when you left, and it stayed with you."

Ash reached for him, cupped his cheeks in his hands, and drew him down. Ash kissed him without reservations, probing deep, tasting him as Brighton did the same. Ash's flavor was the same as before, and in the back of Brighton's mind, he wondered why Ash couldn't see that he was the same. Outwardly he might have changed, but Ash was still the same person he always had been. At least Brighton wanted to believe that. The doubt and pain he sometimes saw weren't part of the man he remembered. They were new, and Brighton was sure he knew the real Ash, the one untouched by the pain and the confusion of confinement.

"Do you have supplies?" Brighton whispered.

"I do, but I wasn't sure if you'd want to do that. I mean…." Ash's cheeks once again reddened.

"Stop with the embarrassment and wonder. You are still my Ash, and I've waited a long time for you to come back to me." Hell, something Brighton never thought he'd have again—a second chance at the life he'd prayed for.

Ash tugged him down once again and rolled Brighton onto his side, then his back, pressing him down onto the mattress. Brighton loved the solidity of his weight, he always had, and the way Ash took charge and guided him—at least he had those first times they'd been together. Brighton wondered if Ash needed him to be the one to do the guiding or if what Ash needed was to be in control. Brighton would gladly do either, and as he was about to ask, Ash took his hands and held them over his head, gazing deep into Brighton's eyes. He had his answer. Ash needed to feel in control, and Brighton stilled. He could give Ash that illusion.

He knew what he wanted, and as the seconds ticked by, Ash grew to want the same things. His fingers explored Brighton's depths, opening to him. Preparation was minimal, but Brighton was aching for Ash's touch, to feel that connection. He held his breath when Ash pulled away, reaching for the nightstand. A rip of foil, some fumbling, then additional slick, and Brighton was more than ready. He'd waited for this for so long, and when Ash joined them together, filling him, he held his shoulders, pressing upward. Brighton wanted more, but Ash seemed determined to go slowly.

Brighton's drive pushed him forward, and he reached for Ash's butt to pull him deeper.

"I will not hurt you."

"Now!" Brighton groaned, feeling the last vestiges of Ash's control snap. He slid deep, to excruciatingly amazing fulfillment, and pulled back, then drove into him again as Ash's gaze seared into his soul. He needed and wanted, and Ash gave him everything he could ask for. This was heaven. Brighton pulled Ash as close as he could, needing, craving as many points of intimate contact as possible. "I love you."

Ash groaned, his eyes crossing. "I love you too, and I'll never hurt you." He stopped, and it was Brighton's turn not to see straight. "And I will protect you in any way I can." He kissed the breath out of Brighton as the pleasure, pure and joyful, built from inside, racing through him like an out-of-control car, then spilled over, carrying them both along in its climactic wake, leaving them bare, breathless, and as content as two people could be.

Brighton lay still, Ash's breathing roaring in his ear, setting the beat of his heart as it slowed back toward normal. Ash pressed closer to him, then rolled onto his side, sighing. "I...." He breathed deeply a few times before trying to talk again. Brighton understood his difficulty; he was experiencing it himself. "That...."

"I know...." Brighton gave up talking and closed his eyes, searching out Ash's lips with his own. They kissed languidly as familiarity for just the two of them descended through the room. This was their time for love to grow, just like it had been before Ash had left. Brighton held his breath a few seconds, and then Ash gently stroked his shoulder, his hand resting at his neck, lightly tugging on the chain.

"You still have it," Ash commented softly.

"The chain you gave me broke a few months ago when Violet grabbed it, so I had to get a new one, but the tag is still there. Other than that, I wear it always." Brighton lay still as Ash fingered the dog tag he'd given him years before on the night they'd first said their words of love. Brighton remembered Ash taking his tag from over his neck and placing the chain with one of the tags around his. It had been just like this, after they'd made love the first time once Ash was home on his first leave, and that tag had become so much a part of him that Brighton didn't even think about it. The chain and the bit of metal rested across his chest and near his heart, where they belonged.

"I'd have thought you would pack it away somewhere." Ash continued fingering the tag. "After what I did, I wouldn't blame you."

"Stop that. Things happen for a reason. Sometimes we don't know what the reason is, and come to think of it, the reason might be completely shitty...." He smiled as Ash chuckled. "I wasn't going to give up what little I still had of you. Would I have moved on eventually? Probably... God, I hope I would have... but I hadn't yet." He stilled Ash's hand, taking it in his. "You're a tough act to follow, and even tougher to let go of." He closed his eyes as Ash carefully shifted on the bed. Seconds later he used tissues to clean Brighton up and then snuggled against him.

CHAPTER 5

ASH DREAMED amazing things all night and then woke to Brighton squirming next to him, pressing his butt to Ash's hips. They'd made love again in the middle of the night and fallen back to sleep in each other's arms.

A crash sent a wave of panic coursing through him, and it took a few seconds before his mind cleared enough that he was back to reality and able to get out of bed and to the hall.

"Aunt Petey?" he called, hobbling to the bathroom to get his robe.

"I'll see if she's okay." Brighton was already up and in his robe, heading past him. He hurried downstairs, and Ash put on his brace and walked toward the hall. "Everything is fine," Brighton said as he came up the stairs a few minutes later.

"Then what was it?" Ash's heart rate had settled back to normal, but he was still on edge. He hated the way he overreacted to normal, everyday things. At least he hadn't gotten transported back to the battlefront or his captivity this time.

"She was on her way to the bathroom and dropped a stack of magazines." Brighton rolled his eyes. "It seems your aunt wanted something to read, and I am not going to go into what that woman has dug up from somewhere in the house and what I had to put back into chronological order for her."

"Dammit...." Ash grinned.

"You know?" Brighton's eyes bugged out of his head.

"Of course I do. Aunt Petey has had a subscription for years, and she likes to be alone to read them. At least she doesn't say something stupid like she reads them for the articles." Ash took a deep breath and turned toward the bedroom.

"Is there something we need to do?"

"Nope. She may be old, but Aunt Petey isn't dead, and if she wants to read magazines with naked men in them, who am I to tell her she can't?" He grinned and broke into peals of laughter, and Brighton followed right behind him. Ash held Brighton, and they continued laughing. "Do you want to know something worse? Imagine her asking me to bring her some into the nursing home."

"Oh God…," Brighton groaned. "What did she do, request flashlights and read them while hiding under her covers?"

Ash had never thought of that, and the laughter began once more. He guided Brighton back into the bedroom and closed the door. The chuckles died away, and Brighton turned to him, his gaze growing more heated by the second. Ash had just opened the knot at Brighton's waist and slipped the robe off his shoulders when a strident knock reverberated through the house. He gasped and stepped back, hitting the door and trying to keep his mind on the here and now instead of taking one of his trips into the past.

"It's fine." Brighton pulled the robe back up with a sigh. "I'll go down and answer the door. It's a Saturday, and I need to get dressed and go to work soon anyway." He looked at the clock beside the bed and then left the room, closing the door quietly.

Ash groaned, wishing they'd had more time together. As Brighton clomped down the stairs, he hunted up clothes and began getting dressed. He managed to get his brace off and some pants on and was adjusting the Velcro straps of the brace once more when Brighton returned to the room.

"There's a man downstairs. He says he knows you from your unit…. I believe him. His bearing screams military. I asked him to sit in the living room and said I'd come get you." Brighton passed him his shirt, and Ash shrugged it on while Brighton dropped the robe he'd been using, pulled on fresh clothes, and gathered up the ones from last night, shoving them into the small bag he'd brought with him.

They left the room, Ash's curiosity and nerves rising by the second. He knew there was most definitely something up. Why, he had no idea, but something was wrong. He could feel it in the air. When they reached the bottom of the stairs, Brighton dropped his bag by the door and they went into the living room together.

Ash's captain sat on the edge of one of the chairs, standing as soon as they entered the room. "Ashton," he said formally, extending his hand. "It's good to see you up and about." He forced a slight smile.

Ash shook his hand, still wondering about this visit. He motioned to a chair as he also sat. "This is Brighton Phillips, a close friend." He turned to Brighton. "Captain Reardon was my company commander." He turned back as Brighton perched on the arm of his chair. Ash appreciated that he stayed close.

"Marty, please," Captain Reardon said much more gently, and Ash wasn't quite sure how to take it. He understood the official tone, but this was almost friendly.

"All right," he said levelly.

Reardon cleared his throat. "I know you have to be wondering why I'm here."

Ash nodded. He hadn't expected to see this man ever again. They hadn't parted on the best of terms, with all the questions regarding their last mission, and Ash blamed Captain Reardon in part for the mess they'd walked into. Distance had mitigated some of those feelings, but not all of them.

"Can we talk alone?"

"No," Ash answered quietly as Brighton's fingers curled into his. "I'm not being dragged back through everything again." God, the last thing he wanted was to review his story yet another time.

"Hasn't he been through enough?" Brighton snapped, and Captain Reardon's eyes widened. "I don't know what you want, but he needs to be left alone so he can heal and rebuild his life." Dang it, Brighton could be feisty when he wanted to.

86

"I'm not here to recall you or to bring you back. You're in no condition, and I think you gave more than your share." Reardon paused and swallowed. "In fact, I'm not here in any sort of official capacity." He seemed a little nervous now, his eyes darting around the room. "Right after your return, my tour came up and I decided to retire. With the way things are right now, I thought I'd get out while I could." He sighed. "I was approached by the NSA, and without going into any details of how, I stumbled upon some information." He shifted his gaze to Brighton and stopped.

"I've known Brighton since we were kids. If anyone knows how to keep quiet, he does." Ash stood and went across the hall to knock on his aunt's door. She called for him to come in, and he peered inside. She was sitting in her chair next to the bed, knitting up a storm, still in her housecoat.

She smiled and put down her knitting. "I'm fine, dear. You meet with your friend and let me know when the coast is clear."

Ash smiled at her and closed the door once again. He returned to the living room and waited for Reardon to continue, now that he was sure they were alone.

"How much does he know about what happened to you?"

"Enough," Ash answered shortly. He had learned long ago to say as little as possible when answering any questions, and he simply wanted Captain Reardon to get on with what he had to say.

Marty nodded and sighed. "I have to start by saying that this conversation never happened, and if anyone should ever ask, I was here only as a friend to check that you were doing okay." He stopped and waited for Ash and then Brighton to agree. "I mean it. This conversation never happened. I could get in some big trouble, but you were one of my best men and I strongly feel that you need to know."

Brighton stood as Ash turned to him. "I'll go into the kitchen and let you talk."

"Are you involved with Ash?" Reardon asked, and Brighton nodded. "Then you need to know this too." He looked serious, which sent Ash's stomach into loops, and he willed the damn thing to settle down. He needed to think and keep a cool head, and he sure as hell wasn't going to jump to any conclusions. "During your debriefing, you mentioned on multiple occasions a man called Musalla. We now know his name is Musalla Hadien. You also talked about his seeming obsession with you."

"Yes." Ash willed his mind not to remember. He could feel the pressure inside his head to go back there and revisit those memories—they pushed at the edges of his consciousness—but he shook them off. He was not going back to that little room from only the mention of his chief tormentor's name. Ash was not going to give him that kind of power. Brighton squeezed his hand a little tighter, and the pressure eased. Ash blinked a few times and his vision cleared, showing Reardon looking at him. "He was just that. Breaking me was his mission."

"I came today because some information crossed my desk by a sort of accident and I thought it was important for you to know." Reardon leaned forward a little and lowered his voice. "This Musalla Hadien had some information that intelligence officials felt they needed very badly. He provided the information, and in order to keep him safe, he was relocated to the United States." He said no more, but the expression on his face told Ash just what he felt of that decision.

Ash's insides instantly felt as though they'd been put in a food processor. His stomach cramped and bile rose in his mouth. He had to force it back down to keep from throwing up.

"They allowed the torturer, my torturer, to come into this country?" Ash gritted his teeth.

"They knew him by a different name. Look, there is only so much information I can pass on. But recently they discovered his other identity, which led them to our old team and what happened to you. Once intelligence officials realized what they'd done, they tracked him down and intended to take him into custody."

All the air sucked out of the room for a few seconds and Ash's head felt light. He hoped to hell he didn't fucking pass out, but he could barely think.

"So you're saying they lost this asshole?" Brighton spat in a stage whisper.

"Yes. When we went to get him, he had disappeared. I don't have information on when he took off or how close we are at the moment to taking him into custody. That's the limit of what I could find out without making anyone suspicious as to why I was interested. But I felt it was important that I alert you to the fact that he is in this country somewhere and on his own." Captain Reardon closed his eyes. "So far off the record, we're in Canada... this is a supreme clusterfuck. If they would have talked to anyone in our area, we would never have recommended this man be settled here, no matter what information he had."

"The right hand has no idea what the left hand is doing," Ash said, unable to get Musalla's black-bearded face, with piercing eyes that he would always associate with hell itself, out of his mind. He had hoped to be able to leave all of that behind him and get on with his life. He'd actually gotten to a point where he could be happy again. And now this. What the hell was he going to do?

"I don't know where he is, and it could be that he simply disappeared before his ruse was discovered. But I can say that he was settled in rural Virginia, about four hours or so from here. I don't know if he knows where you are or anything. But with the internet, it's easy to find out information if you want to search for it badly enough."

Ash nodded slowly. He knew that, and he should be trying to figure a way to find out where this asshole was, but his head didn't seem to be functioning right now.

"What do we do?" Brighton asked.

"I have a picture of him." Reardon handed Brighton a photograph. "And I did a mock-up of what he'd look like without his beard. I figured the first thing he'd do to try to blend in is shave. But I don't know for sure. What I do know is that no one was going to let you know. I think they figured they're going to get him into custody soon. If you do think you see him, call the police and FBI right away. Say that you've seen him and use his name. That should trigger something in their databases, but I can't know for sure. There are too many agencies, and they don't always want to talk to one another. This was supposed to have been fixed after 9/11, but territory and turf are still facts of life in Washington." Reardon stood and shrugged. "I wish I could tell you more."

Ash got to his feet, his leg throbbing, probably in sympathy for his head and gut. "I appreciate you coming to tell us. I really do."

Reardon nodded. "Look, things didn't turn out the way they should have—I know that. And you don't deserve any more grief. Just be safe and watch your back. He'd be stupid to try to come here, especially if he truly wants to disappear, but I think it depends on his ego." Reardon handed him a business card. "I don't know how much I can do, but here's my number in case you need to get ahold of me. Just say you're a friend from my Ranger company, and they should put you through." He headed for the door.

Ash remembered his manners through the fog that seemed to fill the room. "Can I get you something to drink?"

"No. Thanks. I need to get back on the road. I have an appointment to meet some friends in Gettysburg." He smiled, and Ash figured Reardon would use those friends as a cover if anything ever came to light. Not that it ever would through him.

"How about a bottle of water?" Brighton hurried into the kitchen and returned with a cold bottle, handing it to Reardon. "Thank you for telling us. I know this puts you in a difficult position, but you did what was right, and I know that takes courage." Brighton opened the door, and Reardon said a final goodbye and stepped out into the morning air. Brighton closed the door and returned to the living room, looking stunned as he sat on the sofa across from Ash's chair.

"I don't know what to do."

"Nothing for now," Brighton told him. "Just because you found out that guy is out there somewhere doesn't mean he's going to come anywhere near here. He'd be stupid to."

"Musalla isn't stupid. He's cruel and ruthless. He'll stop at nothing to get what he wants. Will he come here? I don't know." Ash had no idea what he was going to do, but he couldn't do anything until he could think straight.

"I need to call my boss and—"

Ash took Brighton's hand. "You need to go on in to work and promise to call me if anything out of the ordinary happens."

Brighton nodded slowly. "Okay. But... I have to work till five, and then my mother will bring Violet home."

Aunt Petey walked into the room, causing both of them to look up. "Are you coming for dinner?" she asked Brighton.

"I don't want to put you out."

"Nonsense," she said with her usual vivacity. "I like having company." She shuffled through toward the kitchen. "I'm going to make some tea."

"Okay, Aunt Petey. I need to take Brighton home so he can get ready for work." Ash got his keys and wallet before pausing and tossing the keys to Brighton. "On second thought, go ahead and take the truck. That way you and Violet can come back after you're done with work."

FEAR REALLY sucked. Once it got started, it took root, and the more one worried or tried to get rid of it, the deeper the damned roots dug. And every time it was pulled out, it came back stronger.

Ash hated fear, but he spent much of the day wondering what he was going to do. To make matters worse, he kept looking out the front windows every time he went into the living room, expecting to find Musalla looking back at him.

"You need to settle down," Aunt Petey told him.

Ash agreed with her, but when he tried, the damned fear returned even more voraciously. In the Army he'd always been taught to use the fear, to push it down and transform it to make him stronger. He kept trying, but it didn't work. Back then they would've been going into battle or on some mission and he would have needed that energy. But this was sitting at home with his aunt, whom he needed to protect, and waiting to see if the one person on earth who had made part of his life a complete and actual living hell was going to return. Fuck, he hoped not.

The soft clang of metal on wood broke him out of his fear-induced haze, and he stared at the gun on the coffee table.

"I've got bullets too. They're in my room upstairs in the stand beside the bed."

"Jesus." He lifted the gun and checked the chambers. "Damn, it's loaded."

"Of course it is. Your uncle taught me how to use it too. Go upstairs and get the extra ammunition from the bottom drawer in my room, and if whoever you keep looking for shows up, blow their fucking head off."

More and more she shocked him.

"I'll get the ammunition in a bit." He carefully unloaded the gun and set it back on the table with the ammunition resting next to it. "Let's hope it won't come to this."

Aunt Petey sat down, placing her knitting bag next to her. "Of course that's what we hope. But we also prepare for what we have to." She went back to her knitting, and Ash thought, not for the first time, that his aunt would have made one hell of a general.

The house got quiet once more, and Ash ran through scenario after scenario, trying to determine what the most likely outcome was. What was most likely was that nothing would happen, but that he couldn't guarantee. No. What he needed to do was leave and set a trail away from here and the people he cared for. Ash was a warrior, or at least he used to be.

He turned his attention to his leg in the brace and the dull pain throbbing in it. There was a time, knowing that Musalla was in the country, that he would have taken the gun Aunt Petey had given him and hunted the man down. But that wasn't in the cards. Everyone would see him coming. No, his best chance to protect the people in his life was to get as far away from here as he could.

Ash stood and picked up the gun and ammunition before heading for the stairs. Aunt Petey would think that he was going to take care of what she suggested, but Ash intended to start packing. He made it upstairs to his room and carefully got under the bed to locate a suitcase. He filled it with clothes and the things that were most important, closed it, and left it on the floor of his closet. Then he retrieved the extra ammunition, put it and the gun on his dresser, and went back downstairs.

"What should we have for lunch?" Aunt Petey asked as he returned to the living room.

"How can you think about that right now?"

She paused her knitting. "I'm hungry. Besides, this man isn't going to show up in the next five minutes." She returned to what she'd been doing, needles clicking quietly. "I also think you should call the police and tell them what you feel you can."

"Were you listening to what we were talking about?"

"No," she answered in a huff. "Your behavior is telling me all I need to know. That man who was here this morning told you something that has you spooked all to hell, and my guess is that it has to do with something that happened while you were gone." Her fingers worked faster, and then she put her knitting back in the bag. "I know you think I'm old and don't understand shit, but I have eyes and I didn't come down with the last shower."

"I never thought that," he said, feeling bad that he'd raised her ire. "I want to protect you from—"

"Ash!" She drew out his name in exasperation. "I am in my eighties, and I've seen a lot more of life than you have. I might not have seen actual combat, but I suspect that has nothing on a ladies' aid lunch. Those gossips could cut anyone to pieces. I don't need you to protect me." She settled back in her chair, and Ash went into the kitchen to make something to eat.

Aunt Petey seemed happy with sandwiches, and they ate in the living room. After they were done and Ash took care of the dishes, he sat on the sofa, wondering what in the hell he was going to do. He lay down, propped his leg up on the far arm, and closed his eyes. He grinned like an idiot as he thought of the reason why he was so tired. At least it took his mind off the bad news from the morning.

Ash was back in the small, dark room, cold even though the room was so hot that sweat beaded on his skin. Fever, he had a fever. Ash tried to will himself better and hoped the sickness would pass. But it hadn't for days.

The creak of the door opening made him jump, and he shivered as his nemesis with black eyes and beard entered the room. "You will tell me what I want to know." He closed the door, and the metallic clang echoed off the walls.

"I don't even know what that is," Ash said, then wished he'd said nothing at all. It didn't matter how many times he denied knowing anything about local troop movements or what future incursions were planned. Musalla was relentless, and Ash was determined to be strong enough to withstand whatever he was going to try next.

Musalla bent down to where he sat, his face close to Ash's. He grabbed Ash's chin with his rough hands and brought their faces close enough that his black eyes, as deep as the depths of hell, looked into Ash's. The shiver from fever increased as Ash glimpsed true and abiding hatred and a complete lack of compassion of any sort.

"Tell me about your family," Musalla whispered, and fear raced through Ash.

Ash clamped his eyes and mouth closed and drew himself to his feet and full height. Everything hurt throughout his body,

94

and he knew his sickness was getting worse. His only hope now was for death. There was never going to be an end to this pain, and every day he was getting weaker. Ash never knew where or when Musalla would strike, and almost instantly Musalla knocked his legs out from under him, and he fell to the rough concrete floor. He bounced slightly, and pain radiated through him, sharp as needles poking every inch of him. Ash opened his mouth in agony and—

Ash woke with a start, nearly falling off the sofa, gasping for air. He blinked, and it took him a few moments to realize he wasn't in that room, and while there was an ache in his leg, there was no sharp pain.

"Are you all right?" Aunt Petey asked.

Ash answered automatically even as his heart pounded and he tried to get that pair of black eyes out of his mind. He knew that hatred intimately and was still experiencing the effects of it. Ash was never going to be free of him, but he couldn't allow the people he loved to fall under his hands. He slowly sat up, propping his leg on the coffee table. His heart raced and sweat beaded on his forehead.

Aunt Petey watched him, and Ash turned away. He didn't want to reveal too much of what he was thinking. "You still having nightmares?"

"Yes. The doctors say they will most likely fade with the passage of time, but that they will be with me for the rest of my life." He tried to keep that in perspective. This was just a dream, a flashback—it wasn't real. That part of his life was over and he could move on. At least that's what the doctors and therapists told him. They'd said to hold on to what was real and the people he cared about. But what if that pain returned? What if the people he cared about were to be ripped away from him?

"I'm going to go outside." He left the room to sit out front, but went upstairs instead. He got the gun from where he'd put it, loaded it carefully, and then carried it back down the stairs and outside.

Ash sat on the porch, the gun on the table next to him with a tissue from his pocket placed over it. He rocked back and forth in the old rocking chair he remembered from when he as a child. Aunt Petey used to sit in it when she was out here, waiting for him to get home from school. Ash gripped the arm of the chair to keep his hand from shaking and looked to the right and left constantly, ensuring no one approached the house without him knowing.

Ash sat there for hours, knowing he was going crazy. His head swam with things that had happened to him in that dank room and the men who hadn't come home from his last assignment. He was still so tired, but when he closed his eyes, even for a second, all he saw was those black eyes staring at him, trying to see his soul so he could take it away. His mind went in circles, endless turning that took him nowhere at all, and the conclusion he kept coming back to, time and again: the only answer was to get away from here and from them.

"MR. ASH!" Violet called as she ran across the yard with a grin on her lips that reached her eyes, papers flapping in her hand. "I drew you something." She bounded up the steps and skidded to a stop at his legs.

"You have to be careful. Remember that Mr. Ash has a hurt leg," Brighton said gently, following more slowly behind her.

Violet gently patted his braced leg. "My mommy used to kiss boo-boos to make them better." She leaned down and kissed his pant leg. Then she raised her gaze and smiled.

Ash lifted her and gently set Violet on his lap. "What do you have?"

"I drew you a picture," she said again, handing him the page. Ash could barely tell what the figures were other than people of some sort. "This is your mommy and this is your daddy. You said they were with my mommy and they were watching out for each other. That's her right up there." Now that she'd said that, he could make out wings. "And this is you with Aunt Petey, and me and Uncle Brighton." She pointed to each one. "At school they asked me to draw my family, and since you said you didn't have one because your mommy and daddy were dead, I added you." She seemed so happy, and Ash hugged her and then kissed her cheek.

"Thank you. This is beautiful. Why don't you go in to show it to Aunt Petey, and once you're done, I'll put it on the refrigerator. My mommy used to put my best drawings there." He hugged her again, and Violet climbed down with his help and hurried inside.

"Aunt Petey!"

Ash smiled. Kids never did anything by halves, and for a few seconds, her joy had overtaken his morose worry. He looked up and saw Brighton looking at the gun on the table beside the chair and then at him, his lips twisting in what Ash hoped was concern and not the precursor to running away in fright.

"How was work?" Ash asked, trying to figure out where he could put the gun out of sight. He wanted it close because it made him feel safer.

"Very busy. We're having a spring cleaning sale and it seemed like everyone in town was in today." Brighton handed him back his keys and sat in the chair next to his. "I spent most of the day worrying about you, and now I see that my worry was well-founded. Are you sitting guard out here?" Brighton smiled and leaned in for a gentle kiss.

"No." Ash brought his hand up, gently cupping Brighton's head so he could take another before he backed away.

"Did you rest today?" Brighton asked, and Ash nodded slowly. "I see."

"What?"

"Your dark expression. You had one of those dreams, didn't you?" Brighton took his hand.

"I'm not broken or a child. Yes, I had a bad dream. So the hell what?" Ash knew he shouldn't have been grumpy, but he…. Dammit, he wasn't sure what the hell he was feeling, and he hated it.

"There's no need to get edgy. I know you have those dreams, and it would surprise me if you weren't having them after Marty's visit this morning." Brighton took his hand. "Do you want to take Violet and me home?" He once again glanced at the gun.

Ash followed his gaze as Brighton bit his lower lip. "I'm just trying to keep us safe." He sighed. "I'm not going to do anything stupid. Aunt Petey gave it to me, and I don't know where she kept the thing, but I brought it out with me." He wasn't going to explain that it made him feel safer.

"What do you think of all this? I know you've had all day to stew on it and chew it over until there's nothing left." Brighton sighed heavily. "I think we should tell the police. They have to know, and they can be on the lookout."

"I can't. Reardon risked his career to come here and try to warn me. If I tell the police, then they're going to wonder how I know about all this, and what am I supposed to say?" Ash groaned. He wasn't one to open up and spill his guts, to anyone….

"You can't hold it all inside," Brighton said so gently, it touched Ash's heart. Why did Brighton have that ability with just a few simple words? He could cut to the quick of what Ash was thinking and worrying about.

"I thought all of this was behind me. That I could come home and try to heal. But the wounds keep opening and I don't know what to do." Ash got to his feet and then sat back down again, swearing under his breath. "I can't even fight."

"I don't know what to tell you, except that there are people here who care for you." Brighton stood and pulled Ash into his arms, holding him tightly.

"I know," Ash said as gently as he could, holding Brighton in return as the answer and what he needed to do settled over him. Surprisingly, the turmoil of the last few hours eased and he could think straight. "I have very good friends now."

"Mr. Ash!" Violet called as she ran out onto the porch. "Aunt Petey says that she has cookies and milk if we want them." She practically jumped up and down. "Are you going to kiss?"

Ash peered over Brighton's shoulder as she made a sour face. "I think so." He brought Brighton's lips to his and kissed him with everything he had.

"Aunt Petey, they're kissing," Violet called inside, and Brighton burst into laughter, his lips still next to Ash's. "And it's yucky."

"I beg to differ on that point," Ash whispered softly and kissed Brighton once again. "Kissing you is definitely not yucky." It was closer to the living end of happiness, if he were honest. He tugged Brighton in once again and put his lips to much better use.

When they parted a few seconds later, Brighton backed away, his pupils huge and his expression glazed. Ash loved that look and knew he'd put it there.

"We should go see about cookies before Violet either eats them all or runs your aunt half to death."

"She's an active little thing," Ash commented.

"Now she is. A few months ago, Violet walked through the apartment on tiptoes, trying to be quiet and not talking. I didn't understand and thought she was a quiet child who didn't like noise. But she got the idea from somewhere that, as long as she was good and didn't make noise, I'd keep her, but if she was loud, I'd send her away." Brighton wiped his eyes. "She finally confessed that to Raymond, and the two of us talked to her." He turned as Violet came back outside with a cookie in each hand and her mouth full. "We'll be right in."

She nodded, swallowed, and took another bite before going back inside.

"She's adorable." Ash was already becoming attached to her. No child should have to go through what she had, but like him, Violet had a relative as amazing as his aunt Petey to look after her. "Let's go inside." His legs were stiff, and it took a few minutes to get the blood flowing once again.

"Mr. Ash!" Violet called as soon as they reached the kitchen. She jumped up and pulled out a chair. "Sit here. That way your leg won't get tired."

He smiled and sat down where she indicated, then gave her a hug as she put a plate with a cookie on it in front of him. She still had two cookies and seemed determined to eat as many as she could get her hands on.

"Only one?" Brighton teased. "Mr. Ash is a big man, and he needs more than one small cookie."

Violet looked at his plate and put down a second one before returning to her own eating. Brighton grabbed a cookie and sat as well, with Aunt Petey taking a place at the table with a cup of tea.

"Aunt Petey used to make the best cookies."

Violet's eyes widened. "You did?"

"Yes." Aunt Petey smiled. "You and I can make some together. Maybe tomorrow if it's okay with your uncle."

"Can we stay the night up in the tower?" Violet asked.

"I take it she's as fascinated with the tower as we were when we were kids," Ash teased, turning to Violet. "The tower isn't comfortable for sleeping, but after dinner, you and Uncle Brighton can go up in the tower and look around. You and Uncle Brighton can stay here if you want. There's a room upstairs that's perfect for little girls. It has flowers on the walls and a white bed with pretty pink flowers on the bedspread."

Violet bounced in her chair, and Brighton leaned across the table. "I don't have clothes for us to stay the night."

Ash ate his cookies and drank the glass of tea that Brighton poured for him. He should have thought of that before he'd opened his big mouth. The thing was, if Violet stayed the night, then Brighton did as well, and that was what he really wanted.

"Ash can take you to get some clothes so Violet and I can have a girls' night." Aunt Petey winked at Violet, who began chanting "girls' night!" over and over without knowing exactly what it meant. Ash wasn't sure either, but he was most likely going to regret suggesting the sleepover without thinking it through.

"Okay. I'll go home and get some clothes for both of us as long as you stop eating the cookies and don't spoil your dinner." Brighton winked at Ash. "I also need to get something to contribute to supper."

Ash handed him back the keys, and Brighton left the house while Violet cleared the dishes one at a time and put them in the sink.

"It will be nice to have a little girl around the house." A dark shadow fell over Aunt Petey's features. "I had a little girl once. She was the only child I was able to carry to term, but she lived just a few days. They said there was something wrong with her heart. After that, your uncle and I stopped trying for children. It was too hard on both of us." She pulled a tissue out of her sleeve and wiped her nose. "It was the one real disappointment your uncle and I had."

"You were never a disappointment to me," Ash told her. He'd always known that he was the child they'd never been able to have, but she had never spoken of her daughter before.

"Or me," Violet added, standing next to her. "So… when is girls' night starting? And what do we do?"

"Well…," Aunt Petey began tapping her finger on her lips as though she were thinking about something. "First, we have dinner and then put on our pajamas. I have games we can play, and then we can tell each other stories and…."

Ash pushed his chair away from the table, leaving the two of them to plan their evening. He collected the gun from one of the high shelves and took it back up the stairs. He put the gun in the locking drawer of his nightstand, then grabbed a duffel bag and packed it with the rest of the things he was going to need. This was the hardest thing he'd ever had to do, but Ash was intent on protecting the people he loved most in this world, and if that meant leaving so they could be safe, so be it.

Ash was well aware that most people would think he was overreacting, but he knew Musalla, and he wasn't going to stay away. For months Ash had been at his mercy, and that wasn't going to happen to anyone he loved. Once he was gone, he'd call some friends and elicit their help in planting a trail away from Biglerville for Musalla to follow. Sure, he might follow it to him, but at least his loved ones would be safe. That was what was truly important.

Ash put the duffel next to the suitcase and closed the closet door. All he had to do when he was ready to go tomorrow was put the things in his truck, say goodbye to Aunt Petey, make sure Brighton would help look after her, and get away from them.

Truthfully, he didn't know if he could do it, but he had to, and the service had taught him that real heroes do the hard things no matter the price. And if it meant Aunt Petey, Brighton, and Violet would be safe, then it was a price he was happy to pay. He'd made his decision and he felt better for it. Resolved once again, he went back down the stairs as Brighton came inside with two bags. He handed one to Violet, who rummaged through it and pulled out her doll and a few toys.

"I brought some salad to add for dinner."

"How about pizza?" Ash asked, and that seemed to meet with everyone's approval, so he placed an order for delivery and set the table. He needed to keep busy for a while.

"Is everything okay?" Brighton asked, pitching in to help.

"Of course." Ash forced a smile and tried to keep his mind off what he was going to have to do. The best thing was for all of them to spend the most time together they could before he had to leave. Ignorance was bliss, and information was on a need-to-know basis—and right now, they didn't need to know. "Pizza will be here in about ten minutes."

"Then you need to put on your pajamas so you and Aunt Petey can have girls' night," Brighton said, glancing over to where Violet lay on her belly, coloring.

She stilled her crayon and looked up at them. "What are you and Mr. Ash going to do for boys' night?" Her question was so intent, Ash turned away, stifling a laugh. He knew exactly what he and Brighton would be doing eventually.

"We're going to watch television upstairs while you and Aunt Petey have your fun down here." Brighton turned to him with a wink. And once again, Ash had to muffle his laughter.

"The boys will be watching sports or something awful like that. But if they're good, we'll let them have some of the ice cream and cookies we're going to snack on. But only if they're good." Aunt Petey winked, and Ash smothered a groan.

Ash had an idea that Brighton was going to be more than just good and that they'd both deserve a treat. Maybe they could sneak upstairs and eat it off each other. That notion sent a wave of heat through him that would melt ice cream from ten feet away.

THE PIZZA arrived, and Brighton made the salad. They ate in the kitchen, the energy simmering between Ash and Brighton so much that Ash's leg ceased aching, or at least he didn't notice it. When they were done, Brighton helped with the dishes, and he and Ash loaded the dishwasher while Aunt Petey got Violet into her jammies. Ash then got a couple of extra blankets and pillows for the sofa before telling them to have fun. He checked all the doors to make sure they were locked, and then he and Brighton went upstairs to watch "boys'" television.

Once in his room, Ash grabbed extra pillows and got comfortable on the bed, turning on the television. He also removed his brace and breathed a small sigh of relief when its weight slipped away and it was just his leg.

"Sometimes I get so sick of the brace and...." He let the complaint die there. Sometimes things were what they were and there was nothing to be done about it, and this was one of those times. He needed the brace, even if it tended to make him seem helpless.

"You won't need it forever," Brighton said lightly as he rummaged through Ash's drawers. "Ah." He turned and handed Ash a pair of soft sweat shorts. "Go ahead and put these on. It'll give your leg a chance to breathe." He bounded to the bathroom, and Ash wondered what was going on until Brighton returned with a bottle of lotion, leaving the door open in case Aunt Petey or Violet needed anything.

Ash got out of his jeans and pulled on the shorts. Then he got comfortable as Brighton gently massaged his leg and knee. Ash leaned back on the pillows, closing his eyes, letting Brighton's magic hands do their work. He had so many scars and didn't like looking at his own somewhat-mangled leg with its patchwork of lines and incisions.

"How is that?" Brighton asked.

Ash croaked out, "Good." He opened his eyes to watch as Brighton let his fingers roam farther and farther up his leg. The damn gray shorts tented, and Brighton was more than well aware of what he was doing. The minx.

"Good?" Brighton snickered.

"You know it is... oh God, right there." Ash groaned as Brighton gently worked a spot that was the source of a lot of the soreness.

"I don't want to hurt you."

"You're not. Oh God." The muscles finally, after days of aching, released their tension, and Ash thought he would come right then and there, the feeling was so damned glorious. He lay back, closed his eyes, and let Brighton's hands continue to work their magic. For the first time in months, many months, he felt human and was pain-free. Granted, Brighton was just rubbing his leg. He wasn't doing deep tissue massage or anything, but this was what he needed. "Can you get comfortable too?"

"Sure." Brighton closed the bottle of lotion and grabbed some light sweats from his bag. He pulled them on and got comfortable next to Ash. Then they found something on TV and sat there together. Every now and again, Brighton would turn to him as though to check that he was still there. He would kiss Ash, just hard enough to keep the heat simmering between them, and then they'd go back to watching reruns of Leonard and Sheldon. Ash was thrilled it wasn't *The Golden Girls.*

They laughed and played a little, getting handsy every now and then. Ash grabbed a blanket from the foot of the bed to spread over their legs, and they got more than a little handsy.

"Brighton," Ash hissed softly, turning toward the door, listening for footsteps. Brighton slid under the blanket and then heated fingers tugged away his shorts, freeing his cock. Ash quivered as Brighton's lips slid around him. "Your niece, Aunt Petey… I…."

"Do you want me to stop?" Brighton stilled.

"No…," Ash groaned feebly, and Brighton took him deep. Ash lay back on the pillows, ignoring the television and everything. Within seconds Ash quivered and the bed shook a little as he did his best to contain the energy Brighton was generating within him. He didn't dare make a sound or move because the bed might squeak, so he sat as still as possible while lights flashed behind his eyes.

Brighton knew just how to play him, building up energy until Ash thought his head was going to explode. Just when Ash thought he was about to tumble over the edge, Brighton slowed and pulled back, giving him a chance to breathe. Then he'd pick up his pace, once again driving Ash toward the edge.

"Is this what you want?" Brighton asked in that tone he had that settled right at the base of Ash's spine and refused to let go, vibrating there like a tuning fork. Before he could answer, Brighton slipped his lips over his cock once more, and he was gone within seconds, past the point of no return. Ash flew into release, mouth hanging open in a silent cry. He knew he needed to make no sound at all, since if he did, it would be a yell that brought the house down around him.

Brighton pulled his lips away and tucked Ash back into his shorts as Ash closed his eyes, floating on clouds of amazement. He lay still, the noise from the television intruding on his peace until Brighton turned it off and settled next to him once again. He brought their lips together, giving Ash a taste of himself on Brighton's tongue.

"If you gave me a few seconds…."

"It's all right. You can take care of me once we go to bed." Brighton leaned against him, and Ash sighed with contentment that he knew could only last so long.

"Uncle Brighton!"

The cry rose up the stairs and straight down Ash's spine. He sat up, while Brighton leaped off the bed and raced down the stairs. Ash followed more slowly, taking care since he wasn't in his leg brace. He used the banister and made it to the living room in one piece.

"He was right over there!" Violet said, pointing. "There was a man right over there, and he was watching."

"She waved at someone, and I asked her to call you," Aunt Petey said. "Probably just someone out for a walk." She nodded and helped Violet get seated on the sofa once again. "Your uncle will pull the curtains."

"Was that man a stranger?" Violet asked.

Ash shared a concerned look with Brighton. "Probably. But he's gone now."

"He went that way," Violet said, pointing again. "Behind the trees over there." She bounced off the sofa and ran to the door. Brighton opened it and she peered out the screen. "He was walking like this…." She did an imitation that was funny. "Sort of like Mr. Ash when his leg hurts." She turned back to Ash. "Is your leg all better now?"

"Not yet. But it's getting there. Your kiss earlier helped." He smiled, and Brighton guided her back and closed the door. "Go ahead and sit with Aunt Petey. Everything is fine, and the man is gone now." Ash locked the door, and Brighton waited while Violet got settled. Ash went into the kitchen, sat at the table, and put his foot up on one of the other chairs.

"I know what you're thinking," Brighton whispered when he came in the room. "Yes, Violet saw a stranger at night, but that doesn't mean it's this Musalla. It could be anyone."

That was true, and Ash's logical brain knew that was a fact, but he couldn't get the notion out of his mind. "I'm not a paranoid person. But I thought he was on the other side of the world, and now I find out he's over here. That's too close for comfort."

Brighton nodded. "If he's on the run, then he isn't going to go anywhere that anyone might look for him. He's going to want to blend in, and he certainly isn't going to come near anyone who might know who he is." He sat in the chair next to him. "We'll deal with things as they come. But we can't jump at shadows and ghosts." He took Ash's hand.

"He isn't a ghost. This man is Satan himself."

Brighton squeezed his hand. "You can't give him that much power. What he is… is nothing at all. He's part of your past, and you can't live there. Doing that just gives him influence in your life, and he's had enough of that." He looked around. "Do you want something to drink?"

"Thanks." Ash knew Brighton was right, but some things are much easier said than done.

107

Brighton brought him a small glass of milk. He took it, his hands curling around the cold glass, but didn't drink right away. "You have friends and family who care about you."

Violet's laugh drifted in from the other room, along with his aunt's.

Ash nodded and lifted the glass to drink the milk, then set the glass on the counter and took a deep breath. Everything told him that his decision was the right one. A last night and then he was going to say goodbye in the morning and put distance between him and all of them.

"Let's check the doors and go on upstairs." Ash carefully got up from the table and joined the girls, who were watching *The Little Mermaid*. Violet was enthralled, which was gorgeous.

"Where did you want her to sleep?" Brighton asked.

Aunt Petey turned to Violet. "Do you want to sleep with me?" she asked, and Violet nodded vigorously. "Could you make up the sofa under the window in there for her? That way I'll be close." She put her arm around her, and Violet hugged Aunt Petey back before returning her attention to the movie.

"Is the bedding where it always was?" Brighton asked, and Ash nodded. He turned to the television, watching the movie, while Brighton hurried up the stairs. He returned with the bedding, went into Aunt Petey's room, and came out a little while later.

"You're all set, sweetheart. I have a bed all made up for you. When it's time to go to bed, I'll come down and tuck you in." Brighton leaned over to gently kiss her forehead. Then he took Ash by the hand and quietly led him back up the stairs.

It took Ash longer than he'd have liked, but he got back onto the bed, stretched out his leg, raising it on a pillow, and watched television with Brighton. He took his medication, and it wasn't long before his eyelids grew heavy. He hated that the stuff made him sleepy, but it was a fact of life for now. He needed the help to control the PTSD. At some point Brighton must have left the room to put Violet to bed. Ash woke when he returned, and Brighton helped him into the bathroom, where he got ready for bed. Then he went back into the bedroom and slipped under the covers.

"They're both in bed, and Violet went right to sleep, holding her doll." Brighton joined him under the covers, and Ash moved close to him. He wished he had more energy at the moment, but the medication had sapped it away. He didn't take it every day, but today had been tough.

"That's good." Ash hugged Brighton and kept his eyes closed as sleep washed over him. Brighton held him in return, and for a few minutes, Ash questioned his decision. How was he going to live without Brighton now that he'd had him in his life again for just a short time? The answer was that he couldn't. Finally he let go and fell to sleep with a smile.

CHAPTER 6

"WHAT IN the hell do you think you're doing?"

Brighton stood at the foot of the bed, hand on his hips, glaring at Ash. He hefted the packed suitcase he'd found in the closet and slammed it on the bed, along with the duffel bag.

"You bastard! You were planning to run." He walked around to the side of the bed as Ash rubbed his eyes. Brighton had gotten up and realized he'd forgotten a robe, so he looked in Ash's closet for the one he'd borrowed before. He didn't find the robe, but he did bash his foot on the suitcase and found it full when he lifted it. "What were you going to tell me?" He was so angry, the words barely made it through his set jaws.

"I...." Ash rubbed his eyes again and reached for the light beside the bed.

"Let me guess." Brighton was in no mood to even let Ash talk. He'd been through this shit before. "We'd make love this morning and then go down for breakfast. Then you'd tell Aunt Petey and me that Musalla was on the loose and that you needed to go. You'd kiss us goodbye, and you might even ask me to look after your aunt... and then you'd be gone. Just like that." He crossed his arms, glowering over Ash. "Tell me I'm wrong."

Ash swallowed, and the dejection in his eyes said that Brighton had been dead-on. "It's for your safety. If he shows up, he's going to do whatever he can to get to me. And that means using you, Violet, and Aunt Petey, as well as anyone else in town that he thinks might be to his advantage."

"Right, so you run away like some coward with his tail between his legs." Brighton turned and then whipped back around. "Dammit! I've been through this shit before, and I'm

110

not going to do it again. You said you loved me, and then you enlisted, and I stood by you. Every time you came home on leave, I was here waiting for you. And then the last time, I thought you were dead. I can forgive you for that and even for leaving when you thought I was with someone else." His voice softened. "But I can't go through that again." Brighton walked to the other side of the bed, realizing he'd been carrying on and was still naked. Ash hadn't said a thing, so he turned to wait for him. "Fucking say something!"

"I thought I was doing what was best for everyone."

"Bullshit. You were doing what was best for you. Things were getting good between us and you and your aunt... so of course you have to run and screw everything up." He smashed his fist into the bedding. "You did before."

Ash sat up. "I had to leave, and you know it."

"Then. You had to leave then, I know that. But you don't have to leave now. You could stay beside the people who care for you and love you." Brighton grabbed his bag and threw it on the bed, pulled out some clothes, and yanked his pants on as he continued glaring at Ash. He had to get out of there. "Ash, you have to decide what you want. I can't go through this again." His anger was slipping away, replaced by fear that he dared not give its head.

"I had decided—"

Brighton cut him off. "You have to know that if you leave, I won't wait for you this time. The last time you left, it nearly killed me, and then when you didn't come home, I nearly died all over again." He wiped his eyes with the back of his hand. "I only survived because of Raymond. But I won't do all that again." He pointed to the bags. "Go if you think you must, but know there's a price, because my heart can't take it again. My parents didn't understand anything about me when I came out... and I came to you. I held on to you all those years. Whenever you were stationed overseas, I worked here and waited for you to come back. Each time you left, I was here, waiting for you. And the last time you left, even though I thought you were dead, I still waited for you. I put my life on hold because I couldn't see a way to go on unless you were here."

"Brighton…," Ash said softly.

"But you know something? I did go on. I'm making a home for Violet. I always ran to you because I thought you were strong and would take care of me. Well, screw that! I can take care of myself. I did it for the last two freaking years, and I'll do it when you walk out that door again. Except when you come back, I won't be here." Brighton yanked the blanket off the foot of the bed, grabbed a pillow, and left the room, closing the door behind him.

It was still dark outside as he made his way to the living room sofa. If it were morning, he'd get Violet and take her home. But she was asleep in the other room. Brighton turned toward the stairs, expecting, maybe even hoping, that Ash would come down and tell him he'd decided to stay, but as the minutes ticked by, the chances of that happening grew less and less.

Brighton parted the curtains, looking out into the night, wondering how things could have gone so wrong. He let the curtains fall back into place and lay down, pulling the blanket over him. It wasn't as though he was going to be able to sleep, and he ended up staring up at the ceiling until he heard footsteps on the stairs. Brighton stilled, afraid to move. He hoped Ash had made his decision, but….

"Brighton," Ash whispered. "Are you asleep?"

"No." Brighton refused to sniffle and wiped his eyes before Ash could see him. His anger had run its course, replaced with worry. He didn't want Ash to go and hoped to all hell that Ash chose him. Brighton knew he had to be strong and prepared to walk away. As he'd said, he wouldn't wait like that again. There was too much heartache in it.

Ash came closer, and Brighton moved his legs over as Ash patted the area and then sat. "I'll never go away," Ash said in the darkness.

"But you were about to," Brighton countered.

Ash sighed. "I was going to leave so that if he was out there, I could drive him away. The authorities are looking for him, and they will find him. Then I planned to come back." Ash patted Brighton's leg.

"How long will that be? And what if he finds you... alone?" Brighton put his hand on top of Ash's. "Then we'd be right back where we were a few weeks ago. I'd be alone once again, and this time you truly would be... dead." The thought brought a lump to his throat. "I can't go through that again."

Ash took his hand. "I know, and I can't expect you to." He brought Brighton's fingers to his lips. "I had decided last night after going to bed that I was going to stay. You and Aunt Petey and Violet are too important for me to leave. But I'm still frightened for all of you."

"You're not leaving?" Brighton asked in a whisper.

"No. I can't. I'm going to choose you. That is, if you'll have me. I know I've made stupid mistakes where you're concerned, and I probably will again. But I'll stay here, and we'll have to fight whatever comes our way."

Brighton sat up, throwing his arms around Ash's neck. He hugged Ash tight, then pulled back to look into his eyes, smirking. "Maybe we should go back upstairs. I don't have to work, because it's Sunday, so there's no reason why we need to get up early in the morning." Full of energy, Brighton slid from under the blanket. "I'll take care of this."

"I'll meet you upstairs." Ash leaned down to kiss him, then stood and headed slowly toward the stairs.

Brighton folded the blanket and grabbed the pillow, checking outside the curtains as lightning flashed and a roll of thunder sounded in the distance. Smiling, he bounded up the stairs and into Ash's room.

The bed had been cleared of the suitcase and duffel bag, and Brighton stripped off his pants and climbed into bed, being careful not to injure Ash's unbraced leg.

He rolled and pressed Ash onto his back. "I think it's time you and I celebrated." Ash had chosen him, and that lightened Brighton's spirit no end. Now he just had to show Ash how much he meant to him.

Ash held still as Brighton lay partially on top of him. Ash's warmth rose up to him, like the heat under a pot on the stove, making Brighton's blood boil. He captured Ash's lips.

After Ash took his lips, tongue possessing him, Brighton whispered, "What do you want?"

"I want to see what all of you tastes like," Ash whispered, his words surrounding Brighton like a blanket. Ash rolled him onto his back and pressed on top of him, his heat growing as his length glided along Brighton's hip.

"You have to be careful of your leg."

Ash chuckled deeply. "I won't be using them for a while." He scoffed lightly. Brighton chirped as he tried to hold in his laughter at what they'd just said, and failed. He threw his arms around Ash's neck and let happiness overtake him. He'd always wanted someone he could laugh with and be joyful with in bed. In his heart he'd known that man was Ash, but for it to happen was beyond happiness. It was joy.

Speaking of joy, passion, and ecstasy, over the next few hours, as the thunder crashed and lightning lit the darkness, the energy from outside filled the room with electricity that heightened what Ash showed him. There was nothing tentative, and when Ash filled him, joining them together, he truly held Ash's heart as Ash held his. It was what he'd waited for all those lonely months, and as the storm outside passed, so did their passion, until they lay together quietly, the rain now gentle on the roof as their hearts settled into a calmer rhythm. It was time for just the two of them, with gentle touches, light kisses, and then arms extended to hold each other until the rain lulled them into sleep.

"UNCLE BRIGHTON!" Violet called, and he cracked his eyes open. Her steps raced up the stairs, and Brighton had just enough time to pull the covers over Ash's bare butt before she burst into the room. She hurried around to his side. "Aunt Petey is making pancakes, and she says to come down or you'll both go hungry." She giggled, and Brighton tousled her hair lightly.

"Go and tell Aunt Petey that Ash and I will be right down."

She was off like a shot, and Ash chuckled as soon as she left the room.

"Faker."

"I was asleep. That girl has one set of lungs on her. Reminds me of your sister." Ash rolled over. "I'm glad you covered me up." He pulled Brighton down into his embrace, and they kissed hard, with passion... and other things... growing by the second.

"You know she'll be back if we don't get up."

Ash mock grumbled and then got out of bed. He limped slightly as he went into the bathroom. Brighton heard the water start a few minutes later and quietly followed him. Ash was singing— off-key, but he was singing—and it was gorgeous.

Brighton slipped off the robe he'd put on, hung it behind the door over Ash's, and pushed the curtain aside. "Is there room for me?" He stepped in front of Ash, the water drenching him, and pulled the curtain closed. Ash moved up right behind him, his chest to Brighton's back, and wound his arms around him, holding him tight, and Brighton leaned his head back against Ash's shoulder.

Ash slowly ran his hands over Brighton's chest, and he closed his eyes, letting the water wash over him while Ash sent shivers through him, making his skin come alive with each touch.

"You know we don't have time for...," Ash whispered.

"Shhh… I know. Just being here is enough." Brighton was coming to realize that some of life's most intimate and special moments didn't take place in bed but when someone showed themselves to someone else, really let them see, and had them care enough to be seen in return. He turned slowly in Ash's embrace, moving closer as Ash ran his hands down his back to cup his butt.

"You feel so good and, damn, you're hot as hell." Ash leaned in to kiss him. Brighton held on tight, his tongue dueling with Ash's until Ash let him win and he tasted his heated musk on his tongue, sending him into sensory overdrive.

"So are you." Brighton spread his legs farther apart to give Ash access and to make sure neither of them fell. The last thing he wanted was for anything to happen to Ash. The water started to cool, so Brighton turned it off and reached outside the curtain for the towels. He handed one to Ash and stepped out of the tub, then made sure Ash got out okay before he dried off and slipped the towel around his waist.

"What's the rush?"

"Uncle Brighton!" Violet called in a singsong voice.

He cracked the door. "We're on our way down," he called back, rolling his eyes at Ash. "Do you want to ask that question again?" He wiggled his eyebrows and hurried out of the bathroom to dress as quickly as he could. Ash needed to put on his brace, and Brighton left him to get dressed, because if he knew Violet, she was going to be back up in about thirty seconds.

Brighton found Violet on the sofa, looking out the front window. "Are you ready for breakfast?" He scooped her up, carried her into the kitchen, and deposited her into a chair. Aunt Petey had batter and a pan all set, but she still looked a little tired, so Brighton offered to make the pancakes, and she smiled her agreement.

"I want to do things but don't seem to have the energy all the time."

"It's all right. You did the important part." Brighton remembered her pancakes. She always made the batter from scratch, and there was something special she did, but Aunt Petey would never say what it was. Brighton made sure the pan was hot and began spooning out the batter the same way he'd seen Aunt Petey do it. He must have met with her approval, because she smiled and quietly left the room.

"What are you looking at?" Aunt Petey asked, and Brighton peered around the corner in time to catch Ash as he turned away from the window.

"Just making sure no one is watching the house." He came into the kitchen after Aunt Petey, his eyes wide, and Brighton could tell he was as tense as a bowstring. "I think, after breakfast, I'm going to take a walk outside."

Brighton shared a brief look of concern with Aunt Petey, but neither of them said anything. If checking things out in the yard made Ash feel better, then that was fine with him.

Ash sat down, facing out the large kitchen windows to the backyard, and Brighton plated up the first batch of pancakes, giving Violet two small ones and putting larger ones in front of Ash.

"Yummy," Violet said. Ash helped her with the syrup, and she dug in.

"You told him the secret and not me?" Ash asked his aunt, who only smiled.

"The only secret is putting the blueberries in each pancake so the batter doesn't get funny," Aunt Petey said as Brighton made a second batch. He wasn't the world's greatest cook, but he liked it, and it was fun cooking for Ash, who had the appetite of a horse today. He wolfed down his pancakes, and Brighton gave him another after giving Aunt Petey a portion. Then he made up the last of the batter for himself, with one more small one for Violet, and sat down to eat when they were done.

In between bites he watched as Ash fidgeted in his seat, continually looking out the kitchen window or angling so he could see through the house. Brighton said nothing and let him work through his security issues.

"I'm going outside. I'll be back." Ash got up and went upstairs. When he returned, fully dressed in dark green camo, Brighton rolled his eyes. Ash leaned down to kiss him, and something hard and cold brushed against his arm.

"Be careful," Brighton told him and let Ash go. He knew this was the result of the conversation they'd had in the middle of the night.

"I'm all done," Violet said, grinning, and Brighton wiped up the syrup she'd spilled.

"Go wash your hands and then you should get dressed. Do you need my help?"

"No."

Dang, for a second she sounded like a teenager. She hurried off to the bathroom.

Brighton watched her go, then turned to Aunt Petey, sitting across the table.

"Did he have the gun?" she asked.

"Yeah." Brighton wasn't sure what to make of that.

Aunt Petey sighed. "I gave him the gun because I thought it might make him feel better. He didn't tell me what was going on, but I know he's upset and anxious. I didn't think it would turn him into G.I. Joe."

"It didn't." Brighton watched as Ash slowly walked the edge of the property. His legs were going to be killing him when he came in, and Brighton figured he was going to need to massage him again. Not that getting his hands on Ash was a bad thing. "I think this is the result of what happened to him." He shook his head, wishing he could do something to help.

"I know. It's beyond all of us." She turned to watch Ash as well, and Brighton stood to clear the dishes. If he was wrong and Musalla was trying to find Ash while Brighton made him do nothing, Brighton would never forgive himself. No, he had to trust that Ash knew what he was doing.

He put the plates and silverware in the dishwasher. Violet came in, and it was obvious she'd dressed herself. "Go see if Aunt Petey can help you get your shoes on the right feet." He figured there was no harm in her otherwise dressing the way she wanted, and by the time he was done, Violet had gone to play. He finished in the kitchen and helped Aunt Petey into her chair in the living room.

"Did you sleep okay?"

"The storm woke me up and I had trouble getting back to sleep. It's usual for us oldsters." She picked up her knitting, and Brighton handed her the television remote. He needed to go upstairs and then gather Violet's things to go home. He didn't want to impose on Ash and Aunt Petey's hospitality.

BRIGHTON GOT their stuff together and helped pick up around the house, going to the windows occasionally to see where Ash was. Finally he heard the back door open and the alarm beep as Ash reset it. Then Ash limped into the living room and dropped into one of the chairs. Aunt Petey quietly took Violet to the kitchen.

"Did you find anything?" Brighton asked.

"No, but the rain could have washed almost anything away."

"What was the sand for?" Brighton asked. "I saw you digging in the old sandbox in the corner of the yard."

"I put it under the windows so I could see if anyone tried to get in. I also set up a few motion detectors. I hooked them into the alarm system so we'll know if anyone approaches the house." Ash sighed and carefully rubbed his knee.

"And you spent too much time on your leg," Brighton scolded lightly, sitting down next to him and undoing the Velcro until the brace fell away. Then Brighton gently massaged the leg through his clothes to try to help.

"You do what you have to," Ash said in a tone that sent a chill running down Brighton's spine. He hadn't heard Ash speak like

119

that, ever. This had to be a part of the soldier inside him coming out. Brighton ignored it and did his best to try to help his leg. "What are the bags by the front door?"

"Violet and I will need to go home." Brighton raised his eyebrows and gently patted Ash's leg. "She and I can't stay here and sponge off you and your aunt."

"I want to sleep with Aunt Petey again," Violet said, putting down her crayons and racing over to jump up and down in front of Brighton.

"We need to go home, and you will need to go to school tomorrow." Brighton thought it best to be firm.

"Can I talk to you?" Ash put his leg down, carefully stretching it out in front of him.

Thankfully Aunt Petey set her knitting aside and got to her feet. "Sweetheart, why don't you and I go sit in the kitchen? You'll have more room to color." She waited while Violet gathered her papers and then led her into the other room. "That way these two can talk about dull boy things." She turned and winked as she guided Violet out of the room.

"Sometimes I swear she has ESP."

"Your aunt knows you really well," Brighton told him. "So what's going on?"

"We need to get out of town. All four of us need to leave. We could find a place somewhere to hide out for a few weeks. Maybe somewhere with a lake for Violet, but it's best if we aren't here in case Musalla shows up." Ash leaned forward, his eyes wide and seeming a touch wild.

"You said you didn't find anything, and I've been giving this some thought. Marty shouldn't have said anything to you... right?" Brighton knew Ash wanted to ensure they were safe in case something did happen. "Isn't going on the run just a slight overreaction? We don't even know if he's anywhere near here." Brighton took Ash's hand, hoping to soothe him, but he wasn't going to go hide in some out-of-the-way place with a five-year-old girl and Ash's eighty-year-old aunt. That was way over the top. "I know you're concerned, and I intend to be here with you, but running away isn't the answer."

"But it will keep all of us safe. We can go off the grid and lie low. Once the authorities catch him, we'll come back. It isn't like I'm talking about spending months away from home." Ash's tone was as reasonable as anything, but the idea was too much. "I want to keep all three of you safe." He pulled Brighton into his embrace, holding Brighton tightly around the waist. "That's the only thing that matters."

"Ash." Brighton ran his fingers through his soft hair. "What about my job and the apartment? What about Raymond? He has a job too. Do we take him along? How about his friends, or Violet's friends? He could use any of them to try to get to us." God, he hoped he was getting through to Ash. Seeing him this way was frightening. "Let's try to be reasonable."

Ash shook his head, and Brighton waited to see if anything he'd said had gotten through. Something told him that a gentle but firm approach might work. Fighting him was only going to make Ash dig in his heels, and that wasn't going to get anyone anywhere.

"Will you and Violet move in here for a while?" Ash asked. "That way I can be with you and protect you."

Brighton closed his eyes in thankfulness. "I'm not sure. Staying with you could turn out to be such a hardship." He let the teasing fill his voice. "Violet likes it here, and I think your aunt likes having her." But he didn't want to impose, no matter the reason. This was Aunt Petey's house, after all. "You will need to ask her permission."

Ash nodded and then looked up at him. "Can you use a gun?" Ash's lips were set and his eyes as dark and cold as steel.

"You know I can. You taught me when you came home on leave, remember? We went to a shooting range, and by the end of our time, I kicked your butt, if I remember." Brighton grinned because they both knew that was a lie. Ash was an amazing shot, though Brighton hadn't done that badly.

"Then I'll show you where the gun is and go over how to load it. If you need it, use it without hesitation. If someone is trying to hurt one of us, it's what you have to do." Ash stared at Brighton and didn't look away or soften his gaze until he agreed. "You should pull Violet out of preschool."

"She just has a few weeks left, and she loves school. They have a specific list of people who are allowed to pick her up, which includes Raymond, me, and my parents. I'll call the school and make sure the list is current and still in force. The teachers all know all of us by sight, and they won't let any child go with a stranger. The play yard is fenced and monitored." Brighton narrowed his eyes, unwilling to budge on this. "We can't become prisoners. We will take precautions, and when I'm at work, I'll pay attention to the people around me, but just like Violet needs to go to preschool, I need to go to work."

"Then I'll drop you off and pick you up. At least I'll know you're all safe."

"Fine." Brighton fingered Ash's shirt. "But you can't wear this." He leaned close. "Though you do look pretty hot, going all commando on me." Brighton snickered as he wondered if Ash had indeed gone *commando* under the camouflage.

Brighton really doubted that this guy was going to come anywhere near Ash—he'd be a fool if he did. Musalla was wanted and was going to stick out. Not only that, but the people who were looking for him were the kind of people who Brighton suspected could bring down a whole lot of hurt. Hell, when they found him, Musalla would probably disappear, and God knows where he'd ultimately end up. No, he was going to go where he had friends or where no one would look for him. But Ash clearly didn't agree with him, and Brighton wasn't sure enough in his convictions to really be able to argue with him... at least not about everything.

"I'd be happier knowing everyone was here where I could keep an eye on them, but as long as you stay in the store with other people around you—"

"Ash, I'll be fine. People come in the store all the time, and we have security cameras. I'll watch out for anyone who looks like the guy in Marty's photographs, and I'll call you and the police if I see anything."

"I wish you could carry a gun at work," Ash said.

"I don't have that kind of job." Brighton patted Ash's hand. "You're going to keep Violet and me safe. But at the moment, we don't have clean clothes here, so if you want us to stay, you need to talk to your aunt, and she needs to be able to make an informed decision." Heck, he was excited about staying here with Ash, but he was worried too. Ash seemed to be going overboard with the security in his reaction to what had happened.

Violet raced back into the room and tried to jump onto Ash's lap.

"Give him a few minutes, okay?" Brighton said as he lifted her into his arms and carried her to the sofa. He sat with her on his lap and turned on the television.

Ash put his brace back on his leg and joined his aunt in the other room. Brighton expected that they'd talk there, but Ash returned to the living room with Aunt Petey and got her settled in her chair with her knitting.

"I want Violet and Brighton to stay here for a while," Ash said, and Brighton rolled his eyes. Putting her on the spot was not what he had in mind.

"Does this have to do with your visitor from yesterday?" She picked up her needles and started clicking away.

"Yes. I want to make sure Violet and Brighton are safe, and I can do that better if they're here."

"Of course they can stay if they'd like to." Aunt Petey smiled, lowering her needles. "I'm assuming that we don't need to make up an extra room for Brighton?"

Violet shook her head. "They sleep together."

"Why don't you go into the dining room and color so we can talk," Brighton whispered to Violet, hoping she'd do what he asked. He didn't often ask her to leave the room, and she seemed to understand this was important. She nodded and hurried into the other room.

"Is this really okay?" Brighton asked as Ash sat next to him and took his hand.

"Of course, sweetheart. Anyone who makes Ash as happy as you always did is welcome here." Aunt Petey turned to Ash. "Do you really think we're in that kind of danger?"

Ash paused. "I do. I think that he's out there somewhere, and…." He put his hands to his head. "I can't do anything if I don't know that all of you are safe. The house is alarmed, and I have things triggered to alert us if anyone approaches. I'll take Brighton to work, and we'll make sure Violet gets to and from preschool and then day care once the school session is over." To Brighton, he sounded like the soldier he'd heard earlier rather than the Ash he knew.

Aunt Petey met Brighton's gaze with a concerned one of her own. "Of course they can stay." She went back to knitting, and Brighton called Violet, who raced in and this time climbed onto Ash's lap to watch television.

BRIGHTON SPENT much of the day unsure of what to do. Ash kept watching out the windows and made a circuit of the yard once more before taking them to the apartment.

Raymond came into his room as he was gathering clothes to take back to Ash's. "What's going on? Are you moving in with him?"

Brighton sighed gently. "Something has happened that might be a threat to Ash, and he's afraid they'll use me and Violet to get to him." He knew it sounded far-fetched, and Raymond rolled his eyes.

"Overreact much?"

"I don't know. What if what Ash thinks is true?" Brighton sighed. "Besides, I can't help him if I'm not there. You're welcome to stay there as well."

Raymond shook his head. "It'll be nice to have the place to myself. Ethan leaves town in a few days, and this way we can have some time alone here. But you take care and make sure you know what you're getting yourself in for."

Brighton shrugged. "It's Ash. He's—"

"I know, honey, and I can't tell you how happy I am that you have each other again. But you need to be careful. With the PTSD and the flashbacks he's probably having, he might not be the same man you knew before he left the last time. I know you love him and I don't want to rain on your happy parade, but please be careful and keep your eyes open." Raymond hugged him and then left the room. Brighton finished packing his bag, then got one for Violet, along with some more of her toys.

Ash sat near the front window, watching the street until they were ready. Ash took Violet's hand as they went down the stairs, and Brighton carried the bags out to the truck. Soon they were on their way back to the house, with a quick stop for some food while Ash called Aunt Petey to make sure she was okay.

Brighton didn't see anything that looked threatening the entire time they were away, but Ash acted like there were possible enemies around every corner. At the second of the two lights in town, someone pulled up next to him and Ash watched them, one hand gripping the wheel until it turned white, while his other reached down for a sidearm… if he'd had one. Thankfully the light turned green and the other car sped away without a glance their way.

"You need to relax a little," Brighton told him, patting his hand, but Ash either didn't hear him or wasn't able to.

When they pulled into the drive, Ash parked and got out to survey the entire area before letting them open the doors. Then he got them inside and retrieved the gun before setting the alarm and returning outside to check the area.

"I think the stress of this is getting to him," Brighton told Aunt Petey as he watched Ash through the front window. "I understand that he's concerned, but...." He wasn't sure what to say to all this. It felt a little like he was a prisoner in the house. The thing was, he wasn't sure if he was Ash's prisoner or a prisoner of Musalla's treatment of Ash. Memories could be very powerful. Brighton had held on to the ones he'd had of Ash very tightly when he thought he was dead.

The alarm console at the back door beeped as Ash came inside and joined them in the living room.

"Did you find anything?"

"No one has been here." Ash sat down and seemed to relax a little, which Brighton was grateful for.

"You need to put the gun away." Brighton wasn't going to have it sitting on the coffee table where Violet could find it. Ash levered himself out of the chair and found a place on a high shelf nearby. Brighton wasn't going to argue. He knew Ash was stressed, but he was getting more concerned by the minute. "Sit down and relax."

"Where is Violet?"

She raced in and climbed onto Ash's lap. He turned on the television, and they watched cartoons together.

Brighton left them and wandered into the kitchen. He stood at the sink, looking out at the backyard. He wished he knew someone he could call to ask some advice on what he should do. Ash was clearly wound tight as a drum, and Brighton was afraid that as time passed, he was going to get more anxious. Brighton knew he needed to talk to him.

He wasn't afraid of Ash, because he knew, deep down, Ash wouldn't hurt him or Violet, but what if someone did come on the property and Ash, in his heightened state, hurt someone? The last thing he wanted was for the man who delivered the newspaper to find himself staring down the barrel of a gun.

The television and Violet's laughter drifted into the kitchen. It was getting near lunchtime, so Brighton made some egg salad sandwiches and brought them in to where everyone was sitting. He handed a plate to Ash and Aunt Petey before helping Violet sit on the floor with hers.

Once they had eaten, Ash cleaned up, and they spent a quiet afternoon together. It was nice. He still watched out the windows and felt the need to check the area around the house one final time before nightfall, but after finding nothing, he seemed to calm down, which relieved some of Brighton's concerns.

Once they went up to go to bed, Brighton realized he was exhausted. He'd spent hours watching Ash, concerned for him, as well as the fact that the possibility did exist that this guy would come after him.

Upstairs in the bedroom, Brighton got undressed and set his phone to wake him in the morning. He didn't want to be late for work or have Violet late for school, and he had plenty to do to start the week. Brighton cleaned up first, then waited for Ash in bed. When he came in the bedroom in his boxers and nothing else, carrying his brace, which he set next to the bed, Brighton forgot about threats, anxiety, and everything else that had happened that day. Ash's chest glistened, and Brighton raked his gaze over his tawny nipples and then down his ripped belly to his narrow waist, with the rest hidden under cotton, most definitely hinting at what lay beneath.

He lifted the covers, and Ash shed his boxers and got into the bed. Brighton snuggled close, resting his head on Ash's shoulder, hand running lightly up and down his belly. "I was worried about you today."

"I know. I think I went a little overboard, but I won't let anything happen to you." Ash drew him closer, guiding Brighton's head upward and into a kiss that sent shivers of passion running through him. Brighton turned languidly, deepening the kiss as the energy between them ramped up. Ash held him tighter as they kissed, like Brighton was the most important person in the world. Ash quivered under him, and Brighton smoothed his hands over Ash's shoulders and then up his neck to cup Ash's cheeks.

"And I don't want anything to happen to you." He swallowed hard as a well of concern, and fear of losing him again, clashed with the fact that Ash was right here with him and threatened to break the dam he'd built to keep himself under control. "But you have to…. God, I don't know. Just…." He held Ash tighter because he couldn't find the words he wanted. Instead, Brighton kissed Ash again and let go of his concern for now. This was a time for the two of them to be together, and he wasn't going to let any threat, real or imagined, interfere with his time with Ash. All other things aside, Brighton understood how precious it was to have Ash back in his life. And a side benefit of a little erotic recreation might help to relax Ash enough that he actually slept. "I want you, Ash," Brighton whispered against Ash's lips.

Ash pulled back just enough that their gazes met, and Brighton bared his soul for Ash. He'd do anything for Ash. Brighton let all the love he possessed show in his eyes, and Ash kissed him harder.

"How do you want me?"

Brighton pressed Ash onto his back and reached to the nightstand. He found a condom, as well as the lube, and set them on the bedding.

"Sometimes I feel so useless. If my leg was 100 percent, I'd…." Ash's words groaned away.

"What?" Brighton breathed as he straddled Ash, then leaned forward. "What would you do?"

"I'd lift you into my arms and throw you down on the bed. Holding your hands over your head, I'd suck on those little nipples of yours until they were peaked hard enough to cut glass." Ash tweaked his nipple with a finger, and Brighton closed his eyes, arching his back into the ting of sensation. "I'd guide you right up to my lips, holding your ass in my hands, slide you between my lips, and take you halfway to heaven."

Brighton rotated his hips forward until Ash pressed his hands to his ass. He continued forward until Ash took him between his lips. He leaned forward, holding the headboard, and Ash sucked him hard. Brighton's eyes crossed at the rhythmic pressure. He tried to hold himself off because Ash had said halfway to heaven and he wanted desperately to know what would happen with the other half. But Ash made him feel so good, he didn't want this to end. Brighton rolled his hips slowly, adding just the right amount of sensation, and he was over the moon. When Ash pulled away, Brighton looked down, his cock hovering over Ash's swollen lips, and he nearly came just at the sight. He rolled his hips back and slid down Ash's body, shaking a little until Ash held him and brought his lips to his ear.

"Now that you're shaking from my lips, I'd tug that little adorable butt of yours into the air and bury my lips between your cheeks, getting you ready for me."

Brighton's mouth went completely dry, and he held still to keep from flying to pieces.

"And once you screamed in frustration, I'd slick myself and sink deep into that tight, hot body of yours, taking you, making you mine forever." Ash kissed him. "Because you are mine. You always will be. I was on the other side of the world, and you were with me. You never left my side in all those months, and through everything, I could never give you up. If I had, I would have lost my hold on what was real. Because you're what's real in my life." Ash pressed his hips upward, and Brighton rolled his, sliding Ash's cock against his backside.

"I can make part of that come true." Brighton reached for the slick and opened it, hands shaking. He hastily prepared himself and then got the condom. He was hardly able to get it rolled down, he was so filled with anticipatory energy. Once he fumbled the damn thing down Ash's length, he slicked it as well and sat back, guiding Ash deep inside him. Brighton sighed when his ass reached Ash's hips. He held still for a few seconds before leaning forward. "Now, make me yours." His heart swelled, and he felt it meld with Ash's.

Ash wound his hands under Brighton, cupping his butt, holding him as he set the pace for their joining.

Time seemed to stand still for Brighton. He lost himself in Ash's eyes and what Ash was doing deep inside his body. This was worth waiting months for, years, a lifetime. This was love, and he and Ash had all night to—

An alarm went off, piercing his thoughts, surrounding them like the siren in a prison to warn of an escaping mass murderer. Brighton jumped, Ash sliding out of him. Brighton came down hard on the bed, grabbing the pillow to shield his ears from the piercing sound.

CHAPTER 7

"Fucking hell," Ash swore as he got up and pulled on a pair of pants. He hobbled out into the hall, found the upstairs console, and silenced the ear-piercing shrill. His head still rang from the noise, and he got his brace on his leg as Brighton, in a robe, hurried past him.

"What the hell happened?" Brighton asked as he clomped down the stairs.

Ash dressed in record time and stepped into his boots before going downstairs, where he found Brighton, holding a crying Violet, and Aunt Petey standing in the doorway to her room.

"I'll check out what's going on." Ash got the gun from where he'd put it earlier. All of the doors showed as closed on the console, so it must have been something outside that had triggered the alarm. He hurried through the house, wishing he could move the way he did before all this shit happened.

Ignoring the soreness in his legs, he went out through the garage and locked the door behind him, then headed into the backyard. His senses on overdrive, he picked up every sound—the rustle of leaves, a twig snapping off to the right. He slowed, staying low and in the shadows as he made his way to the far corner of the house.

The tumble of a metal trash can rang through the night. He closed his eyes for a second and was back in the heat and sand, sweat pouring down his back. He was with the men in his unit, but none of them said a word. Another bang, and he was instantly on alert, his heart racing. He stopped and blinked. Ash needed to be in the here and now, not taking trips into his disturbing past, but it was hard. All around him the scents and sounds of the night tugged at him, pulling him away. He breathed deeply, blinking, forcing his mind to concentrate on what was around him now. Ash stopped, listening for each noise. Once he heard the rustling again, he approached the corner, gun ready.

"Don't move!" he demanded with all the energy he had, pointing his gun, ready to pull the trigger.

He stared down the barrel at a family of racoons.

His heart pounded in his ears and he blinked, making sure this wasn't his imagination and there really wasn't someone there. The raccoons rose up on their hind legs as though they were getting ready to attack. Ash took a step back, still holding the gun steady, not trusting his eyes. They scattered in all directions, heading back for the trees, right past the sensor Ash had set up.

Raccoons. He'd nearly shot a family of raccoons.

Ash leaned against the house, still breathing hard as he listened. Insects chirped, but nothing else moved, not even the animals of the night crawling through the leaves. They were silent, and Ash had scared away the intruders. Too fucking bad he'd awakened the entire house, scared Brighton half to death, made Violet cry… for fucking raccoons.

Ash turned back to the house, looking up at the silhouette against the sky. He had to keep them all safe. That was his mission. If he didn't, he'd lose everything that mattered to him, and he couldn't go through that all over again. Ash pushed it from his mind, checked out his warning system, and made an adjustment so the focus was higher off the ground before going back inside.

He reset the alarm and followed the light to the living room. Brighton sat on the sofa with Violet in his arms, rocking her gently.

"It's all right. That was just the alarm, and everything is fine." Brighton caught Ash's gaze, and he nodded. "There are no bad men out there to hurt you." He continued rocking. Eventually Violet quieted and Brighton took her in the other room. Aunt Petey was sound asleep, and he left the room.

"What happened?" Brighton asked as they climbed the stairs. Ash's leg ached something fierce, and he leaned on Brighton as he went up.

"It was a false alarm."

"Deer?" Brighton pressed.

Ash sighed. "Raccoons. I adjusted the sensors so it won't happen again." God, he hoped not. But it was worth a false alarm to ensure they didn't have a more lethal visitor.

In his room, Ash once again took off the brace, undressed, and got into bed, waiting for Brighton to come out of the bathroom. He expected they'd try to pick up where they'd left off, but Brighton yawned before switching off the light. Ash held him close, but Brighton tossed and turned while Ash stayed awake, staring at the ceiling, listening for any sound in the house that shouldn't be there. He'd put the gun in the nightstand drawer next to him, and that comforted him.

When Brighton rolled over yet again, Ash did the same, pulling Brighton to him and doing his best to try to calm his still-racing heart. In combat he was a master of staying awake and alert for hours. He could sleep and be ready to go at the slightest sound. Finally he let himself drift off, only to awaken when Brighton coughed, and then again a few hours later when a thump from downstairs brought him around again. It was Aunt Petey using the bathroom, but it was enough to wake him.

"Just go to sleep," Brighton said, thankfully sounding still half asleep.

Ash hummed his agreement and held Brighton a little tighter before succumbing to a deeper rest.

The desert stretched out to the right, the city to the left. They had to get in and out as quickly as they could, without raising anyone's suspicions. They knew their target and exactly where he and his associates were. Ash and his unit moved forward with inhuman speed, covering miles in a few minutes. As they approached the compound, shots rang out and one of the men near Ash went down.

The first shot was followed by dozens, then hundreds, all at them. It was a trap, and Ash went to the ground, instantly working out a plan to get them all the hell out of there.

A thud and he was awake, staring up at the bed with Brighton looking down at him from above, his eyes filled with concern.

Brighton jumped off the bed to help him up. "Did you hurt yourself?"

Ash shook his head, blinking. He was in his bedroom, with familiar walls and gentle, helping hands. His blood raced in his ears but quickly settled so he could hear normally.

"I'm okay." He sat on the edge of the bed, holding his head in his hands.

"Hey. It was just a dream."

"A flashback...."

"Call it what you want, but it wasn't real." Brighton caressed his shoulders. "This is real. Me touching you is real. The dream and whatever you were remembering wasn't real. That was the past, and you're safe now." Brighton pressed to his back, holding him tightly, rocking just like he'd done with Violet. "It's all right."

Ash's mouth tasted like the sand from his dream. "Would you get me something to drink?"

Brighton hugged him and then his arms slipped away. He climbed off the bed and returned with a glass of water. "Do you want to talk about it?"

"No." That part of his past would only taint the important people in his life the way it had him. He wasn't going to let them carry this burden for him. His memories and what happened to him were his to bear. "I'll be okay." He took the glass, drained it, and handed it back. "You were right. It was just a dream." He smiled and turned so he could see Brighton. Tilting his head back, he tugged him down into a gentle kiss. Brighton's lips cocked upward, a little crooked, and his eyes read "skeptical" in big bold letters. But Ash really couldn't talk about it. He was already too close to the edge, and if he tipped over and started talking, he wouldn't be able to stop. So he did what he had to and kissed Brighton once more, leaning back on the bed, pulling him down along with him.

"I HAVE to leave for work," Brighton said two hours later. "And I need to drop Violet off at preschool."

Ash smiled and turned away from the window. The rest of the night had been blessedly quiet, and after making love, he'd fallen into a deep and dreamless sleep. "Okay." He finished his coffee and saw to his aunt, who was in her chair, knitting and watching television. "We're going to lunch at Rose's later."

Aunt Petey perked right up. "Okay. I'll stay inside."

"I hooked the alarm system to my phone this morning, so if something happens, open one of the outside doors and I'll know it."

She patted his hand. "I'll be fine. I have my shows and some tea. Don't worry about me. I'm happy." She went back to her television and knitting.

Brighton got Violet in the truck, and Ash drove her to school and then dropped Brighton at work. He called Aunt Petey as soon as he was heading back to the house, which was fine as far as he could tell. Ash made a round outside, checking for anyone who might have approached, but there were no disturbances. But rather than making him feel better, it only increased his anxiety.

Musalla was out there somewhere, and Ash could deal with an enemy who came at him directly. This waiting was making it harder and harder. If he knew how or when he was going to attack, Ash could prepare for it. Right now it was a lot of waiting and nothing else. Ash checked the sensors and the alarm system and made sure his sand indicators remained fresh.

"You need to think about what you're doing," Aunt Petey said when he sat down in the living room a little later. "I know you want us all to be safe, but we can't turn this house into a fortress."

"I'm not. It's just until they catch him or I take him out if he shows himself." He turned to watch out the window once again. There was no one coming up the drive, no people skulking in the bushes. "I will not let anyone hurt you." Ash leaned forward, putting his hand on her knee. "I spent all that time in the service and in that filthy room to protect you, for you. I can't let anything happen to any of the people I love. I can't lose you all again."

Aunt Petey put her hands on top of his. "You've never lost us. We've all been here."

"You don't understand," Ash said urgently. "I know you can't understand, but you have to trust me." His hands trembled. "Please just trust that I'd never hurt any of you."

"Of course you wouldn't." She shook her head. "I don't think you're making sense. But it could be me getting old."

"No. It's me." His head ached and he needed to spend some time resting.

"Take your medication and lie down. I'll be here, and I promise to wake you if anything happens."

"I hate it. The stuff takes me out of my head." He sat back, running a hand over his face.

Aunt Petey stood and went into the kitchen. She returned with a glass that she set on the coffee table. "You watch over me all the time. Now, do what you know you need to, and let me watch over you. I did that a lot when you first came to live here. Remember? We used to stay up all night talking, and I held and rocked you many nights to get you to sleep."

"I was so ashamed," Ash admitted.

"Needing someone isn't shame or weakness. It's a gift. It means that you have someone who cares enough to want to help. You remember how you helped Brighton when he needed you? Who got the most out of that? Was it him for needing the help… or you for giving it?"

Ash nodded. "I got Brighton," he said softly. "I fell in love with him then."

136

"Yes. And you got a miracle because of it. You found the other half of your soul. Most people never do that. They look their entire lives, fall in love, get married, and live their lives, but they never have what you have." She sounded so urgent, Ash wondered if something was wrong.

"How did we get on this subject?" His head spun a little at the twists and turns of their conversation.

"Because you always think you need to be strong and take care of everyone. You stand guard and protect all of us. But sometimes you're the one who needs to be protected." She picked up her knitting once again. "Let the rest of us watch out for you every once in a while."

Ash stood and went upstairs to the bathroom. He opened the medicine cabinet and stared at the pill bottles. His leg ached pretty badly. Ash opened one of the bottles and took a pill, then closed the mirrored door before returning to the living room. He lay down on the sofa, ignoring the television as the medication kicked in. He'd just taken something for the pain in order to keep his wits about him, but sleep still seemed to catch up with him.

THE DAYS began blending together. Ash varied his routine, but the week passed with no further incidents, and Ash could feel Brighton becoming anxious and impatient. Still, Ash knew he needed to remain vigilant. Daily, he checked his perimeter and the alarm systems. He continued driving Violet to school and Brighton to work, then picked them both up at the end of the day. Some nights he barely slept as his dreams became more intense, showing him in vivid detail what happened when he let his guard down for a second, boosting his determination.

"Thank God tomorrow is Saturday," Brighton said Friday evening after Ash picked him up.

"Are you kidding? Isn't that your busiest day?" Ash opened the truck door and helped Violet out. She bounded toward the house, and Brighton caught her, letting Ash check on his phone that all the doors were secure. Granted, Aunt Petey was home, but Ash grew anxious each time he had to leave her alone. He always made sure that the doors were alarmed and that she had what she needed so she wouldn't try to go out.

"Yeah. But the owner, Harry, was gone all week, and I've been working extra hard. He's talking about cutting back to just the pharmacy, and I want him to see me as a potential manager for the store." Brighton followed him to the garage door, and Ash deactivated the alarm and let them all inside. Violet beelined for where Aunt Petey sat at the table with a snack of apples and crackers ready for her.

He liked the way all of them felt like a family. Aunt Petey adored Violet, who ran right up to her for a hug and then sat at the table, chattering away while she ate, and Aunt Petey listened to a total replay of her day. Ash leaned down, rustling her hair and wishing this could continue forever. Having a family like this had been his dream. His original vision hadn't included a child, but he was now having a hard time seeing his future without Brighton and Violet in it. All he had to do was love them and do whatever was necessary to keep them safe.

"I'm going to check outside."

Ash hugged Brighton, grabbed the gun, and went outside. He reset the alarm and headed to the lightly wooded edges of the property. The nearest home wasn't far away, but the trees left Aunt Petey's house appearing out on its own.

Everything looked good. There were no human tracks, though there were animal tracks, which was good. If people were watching the house from out here, the animals would have moved on pretty quickly.

A high-pitched buzzing sounded in the distance. Ash moved behind the nearest thick tree, watching the sky above the open space where the house sat. He scanned the sky as the buzzing grew louder. Ash knew that sound; he'd heard it many times in training and in combat. A drone. He continued looking up, and sure enough, there was a flash as the sun reflected off the object. Ash lowered himself to the ground, giving his body as small a footprint as possible.

More buzzing sounded, and Ash clung to the tree, hiding behind it, watching as the first drone was joined by a second and then a third. They hovered in the area, and Ash was unable to move. He'd found him. Musalla and some friends…. It didn't matter who exactly was on the other end of those drones, with their cameras and who knew what else had been fitted on them.

Shifting, Ash pulled the gun out of his belt and sighted it in on one of the drones. It was too far away to get a good shot, but Ash stayed steady, willing the sucker to come within range. If he had a rifle, he'd be able to take out each and every one of the suckers, but with the handgun, he needed them to come closer.

The drones stayed far enough away, and Ash wasn't about to give away his position by taking a Hail Mary shot. So he sat, listening, watching, his heart pounding but his head clear and his senses as heightened as they'd ever been. Ash picked up the slightest change in tone from any of the three drones. They circled the area, staying away from each other, but he could tell by their flight patterns that they were surveying the area carefully. Ash had enough cover with the leaves of the tree that unless one of them was equipped with some sort of heat-seeking technology, he wasn't going to be seen.

He mentally ticked off possibilities as he stayed as still as he could. Finally, after a good half hour, the buzzing softened as the drones moved away. Ash burst from his hiding spot and made for the house as quickly as he could. He opened the back door, reset the alarm, and found Brighton in the living room.

"What is it?" Brighton asked immediately.

"He's found me," Ash answered breathily, excitement—the kind that meant survival on the battlefield and kept his senses sharp—racing through his veins.

"You saw him? Where?" Brighton followed as Ash hurried toward the stairs. He started upward as Brighton took his arm. "What's going on?"

"He's found me, and I need to take action." Ash grew impatient. Time was of the essence, and he needed to move before Musalla got closer to him and his family. He paused a second as the thought burst into his head. Brighton and Violet were part of his family, and one did everything possible for family. Even things someone hated or…. Ash pushed those thoughts aside as he continued upward. He had to get to his room, a plan forming in his head. He had only one choice.

Ash's leg ached something awful. He'd been on it too much, so he used his arms to partially pull himself upward.

"Ash," Brighton called from behind him, but Ash barely heard him. He was on a mission, and his goal and objective were all that mattered.

He got to his room and awkwardly managed to get down far enough to pull his suitcase and duffel out from under the bed. He set the suitcase on his bed and checked that he had everything he needed. He went to the bathroom, retrieved his kit, and placed it inside the case before closing the lid, then turned to leave.

Brighton stood in the doorway, his expression unreadable. Then his lips turned downward, his shoulders slumped forward, and he closed his eyes for a few seconds. "You never believed what you told me, did you?" His words were soft, but they cut through Ash like a knife. "You said you were going to stay, that I meant more to you than anything else." Brighton stepped forward and yanked the duffel bag off the bed, turning away from him. Ash took the suitcase and followed. Brighton reached the top of the stairs and dropped the duffel, watching as it rolled to the bottom. "That's all I'm worth—a tumble."

"If I lead him away—"

"Who? Did you see him?" Brighton demanded.

"I didn't have to. He had eyes in the sky. I know it." Ash's hands shook as he pressed forward.

Brighton stood against the wall, out of his way. "You mean the drones from the men who were testing them today? There were three of them, weren't there?" He sighed. "They stopped in the store because they needed batteries, and I helped them. They were testing out their equipment because they got special permission to fly them over the battlefield tomorrow as part of a research project. And none of them look anything like the picture Marty gave me."

Ash breathed deeply and blinked, letting this information settle into his adrenaline-drunk mind. "Researchers? And you saw them?" His head swirled as the notion of what he knew was replaced by fact.

"Yes. I saw them."

Ash let the suitcase fall from his hand.

"There was no threat. They were just people testing out their equipment."

"They were over the house."

"It's an open area, and they were probably testing their cameras and needed something to see." The words were understanding, but the tone was anything but.

Ash turned as Brighton pushed away from the wall and went back into the bedroom they'd been sharing for the last week, closing the door. Ash hesitated, then followed him inside.

Brighton had his bag on the bed and was putting his things in it. "Raymond, can you come get us?" He had the phone propped to his ear, holding it in place with his shoulder. "I'll explain everything as soon as you get over here, but I need to go home... now." He waited, then ended the call, put the phone in his pocket, and closed the bag. He turned around but said nothing to Ash as he hurried past him down the stairs.

"What's going on?" Aunt Petey asked when Ash reached the top of the stairs to start his descent. His leg throbbed now and the stairs seemed daunting.

"You're going to need to ask Ash," Brighton answered gently.

When Ash got halfway down the stairs, Brighton's bag was already by the door.

"Go ahead and put your toys in here. Can you do that for me? You and I are going home. Uncle Raymond misses us."

The break in Brighton's voice reached Ash's ears, and he managed to make it to the bottom of the stairs. By the time he reached the living room, Brighton passed him with Violet's bag, set it next to his own, then returned with the toys and finally Violet herself.

"I'll miss you, sweetie," Aunt Petey said, hugging Violet as she looked over her shoulder at Ash.

"We'll miss you too." Brighton leaned down to kiss Aunt Petey's cheek and then held her hand for a second before pulling away. He went to the door and opened it. The alarm console began to beep in the kitchen, but Brighton ignored it. "Can you carry this bag?" he asked Violet, who picked up her toys. She turned and waved to Ash. Brighton didn't look at him as he picked up the other suitcases.

"Brighton…," Ash said, stepping forward to try to stop him. The look he received would have turned him to stone if that were possible.

Brighton stepped outside and closed the door again as the alarm inside the house started blaring.

Ash hurried to the kitchen to turn it off, and by the time he returned, Brighton and Violet were gone and Raymond's car was backing out of the driveway. Ash let the curtains fall back into place before turning to Aunt Petey.

"What in the hell did you do?" she snapped with a vehemence Ash had only heard a few times in his life. "You really messed this up, didn't you, boy?" There was no sign of the sweet, loving person he usually knew in that thin, frail body. Instead, the tiger staring back at him left him cold.

"I was trying to protect all of you," he answered dejectedly before collapsing onto the sofa.

Aunt Petey leaned forward, looking through to the hallways and then back at him, shaking her head. "Why in the hell would you think that leaving would protect any of us from anything?" She glared at him, then picked up her knitting needles. "You have a really fucked-up sense of how to protect someone."

CHAPTER 8

"BRIGHTON," RAYMOND said gently as he placed a plate of scalloped potatoes and ham in front of him. Violet sat on the other side of their small table.

Brighton smiled his thanks to Raymond and waited for him to sit down before starting to eat. "I have to work late tomorrow night," he said, and Raymond nodded.

"I'll pick up Snicklefritz here from preschool, and we'll play games and stuff until you get home." Raymond tickled Violet, who giggled. Brighton needed her laughter and happiness right now.

"Can I go to Aunt Petey's?" Violet asked, as she had almost every night for the last three days.

"Honey, I have to work, so Raymond will pick you up. If you're good he'll take you for ice cream." Brighton wasn't above distraction and bribery if necessary, and ever since he and Violet came home, he'd used the distraction thing more and more.

"Yay!" Violet returned to her meal, eating it slowly, one small piece at a time, as though she was still trying to figure out if she liked it or not.

"It's good, isn't it?" Brighton pressed, and Violet nodded, eating a little faster. He turned away, letting his smile fall from his lips. He was so tired of forcing himself to appear happy. But he needed to, because he didn't want to upset Violet, and Raymond didn't deserve to be around a Gloomy Gus all the time.

It was his own fault, after all. He'd believed Ash when he'd said that he was going to stay and see things through. And he felt like a damned fool. Ash hadn't intended to stay at all. He'd kept his damned bags packed so he could run at any time. Brighton hated how depressed he was, but he also felt betrayed. For years he'd seen Ash come back into town, only to leave again when he had to go back on duty. That was part of the deal, but once Ash's time was up, he was supposed to come back home and settle down with him, making their plans come true. Then Ash left him the last time and didn't come back for twenty-one months.

Brighton pulled his mind away from rehashing old news. He'd forgiven Ash for what happened, because he believed him and thought that they were going to start again. He was a fool.

"Do you want to talk about what happened?" Raymond asked.

"Uncle Brighton threw one of Uncle Ash's things down the stairs. It went bump, bump, splat." Violet grinned and took another bite. "I saw it."

"You did?" Raymond said, turning to him, eyebrows raised.

Brighton looked down at his plate and ate what he wanted before sitting back, drinking some coffee, and closing his eyes. He really didn't want to talk about it. Being made a complete fool by someone he loved and thought loved him back wasn't something he wanted to hash over again.

"Are you done?" Raymond asked Violet. "If you are, then wipe your face and hands and you can watch some cartoons." He stood and got her settled in front of the television with Disney Junior before returning to the table. "Brighton."

Damn, he hated when he used that tone. "Raymond...." Two could play that game.

"You need to get whatever happened off your chest." Raymond cleared the plates and took them to the kitchen. "I cooked, so you do dishes."

Brighton nodded and went in to start the water in the sink.

"Are you sick?" Raymond put his hand on his forehead, and Brighton didn't object. "You hate dishes."

He shrugged and squeezed in a little dish soap. "I loved... love him, and I thought he loved me. But as soon as things got tough, he was ready to run... again." Brighton began washing the glasses and set them in the drainer to dry. "I.... Am I that awful and that big a loser?" He blinked.

"You aren't a loser," Raymond said, more loudly than was necessary, though Brighton appreciated his conviction.

"My parents pushed me away when I came out, and it took weeks for them to take me back, but things were never the same. Through that and the fact that my father still doesn't talk to me much, Ash was there. I thought I could rely on him. Then he left me too."

"He was captured," Raymond reminded him, being the voice of reason that Brighton didn't have much use for at the moment.

"And he stayed away for another year without saying anything because he jumped to the wrong conclusion. He left me alone to grieve for him for a year. And he was going to do it again… and again. How many times do I need to be hit over the head before I realize I'm not worth it?" Brighton wiped his eyes on the arm of his shirt. "I'll be fine. Just go do what you need to and let me finish these and cry into the soapsuds like some heartbroken teenager. Maybe I'll feel better after that." He forced a smile, and Raymond put his arms around his waist, holding him.

"It will be okay," Raymond said, resting his head on Brighton's shoulder.

"I know it will be. I need some time to process all this. It's been a bunch of highs and lows, and maybe you're right. This roller coaster ride needs to end." Brighton really didn't believe a word of it, but if it made Raymond feel better and gave Brighton a little internal fortitude, then maybe that was a good thing.

"Just tell me what happened," Raymond whispered.

Brighton sighed. "Before we went to stay at Aunt Petey's, we got some news. I can't go into it. But Ash wanted to run, and I found his suitcases…." He shook his head. "He promised me he'd changed his mind and was going to stay. Ash promised me, but then, as soon—" Brighton swallowed so he could talk. "He never intended to keep his promise. Ash had bags packed under the bed, ready to run the entire time. He didn't believe in us enough to stay." And that's what hurt the most.

Raymond let his hands slip away. "Did you believe in the two of you?"

"What the hell?" Brighton turned around, soap and water dripping on the kitchen floor. "I waited for him and held a torch for him for almost two years, I missed him so much. I guess I think he should have missed me and wanted to be with me." He turned back to the sink, noting he'd have to clean up the floor once he was done. "You're supposed to be on my side."

"I am on your side," Raymond told him. "But I get the idea that you expect Ash to be the same person he was before he left, and he isn't. Ash is a different man because of what he went through."

Dammit. Brighton hated it when Raymond was so logical and pointed out the flaws in his behavior. "So I should have stayed and let him go…."

"I didn't say that. You can't control Ash and what he does. All you can do is manage your own expectations, and I think you expected that, after a little, things with Ash would be like they were before. But they can't be. You have a daughter now, and he's… God, I can't begin to think what he's gone through." Raymond picked up a dishcloth, dried the floor, and then tossed it aside before getting a clean one.

"I gave up too soon?" Brighton hated that he second-guessed everything.

"He made a promise and then went back on it. Would Ash have done that before?" Raymond asked, picking up one of the glasses from the drainer to make room so Brighton could add the plates.

"No. He always kept his promises. That's what I don't understand." Brighton started washing the pans, then rinsed them and placed them on the drainer when there was room. Finished, he let out the water. "How could he change that much? Sometimes it's

147

like I don't know him, and other times he's exactly the person I've always loved." He was so confused, wondering constantly if he'd done the right thing. "I told him if he left, I wasn't going to wait for him again."

"I know, and I don't blame you."

"And there's Violet to think about. I can't have someone in my life who isn't going to be steady." He turned to where she sat on the sofa, laughing along with the cartoons. "She's already lost too many people, and I can't have a revolving door of guys in and out." But the truth was that he just wanted Ash. He'd been in love with him for as long as he could remember having those kinds of feelings. Ash was the other half of him.

But then a thought occurred to Brighton. What if he wasn't the other half of Ash? Maybe that was the issue. Not that it mattered.

Brighton cleaned up the kitchen, turned out the lights, and joined Raymond and Violet in the living room. This whole situation really sucked. Violet watched her cartoons and laughed, and Raymond played with her while Brighton wondered what Ash was doing and where he was. More than once he'd been tempted to ask Raymond to drive by Aunt Petey's just to see if Ash was home. Brighton didn't want to see him, but he wanted to know he was okay. Hell, who was he fooling? He missed him so hard, it ached. Brighton turned to Raymond and knew in an instant that he wasn't fooling him for a second.

"We should find something else to do," Raymond pronounced.

"Once this show is over, you can play with your toys for half an hour, and then it's bath time." At least their routine gave him some comfort.

"But I just wanna watch some more." She pointed to Mickey Mouse.

"When this show is over," Brighton said gently, standing his ground. "We'll play with you, and then it's time to get ready for bed." It was so easy for him to be short with her, and Brighton needed to remember that it wasn't her fault he was miserable.

Brighton sat still, letting Violet watch. Eventually he closed his eyes, and his mind drifted almost instantly.

"I know enlisting isn't what you had in mind for us, but I need to do this." They sat up in the treehouse they'd built together. It was going to need to be torn down soon or else it would fall apart come winter. But it was hard to give it up since it was their spot... sort of. *"I'm smart and strong, and I'm going to join the Rangers if I can. They're the best, and that's what I want to be. Once I'm done, I'll come back and I'll have savings so we can get that house we want."* Ash took his hand and tugged him closer. *"I'll be home on leave, and maybe if I'm overseas, I can arrange to take leave there and you can come to see parts of the world."*

"That would be awesome." Brighton hadn't seen anything outside of central Pennsylvania. Travel was something his family never did. *"I'm going to miss you. But I'll be here when you get back."*

"You won't find anyone else?" Ash asked, his eighteen-year-old eyes so full of light and energy.

"There will never be anyone else for me but you." Brighton leaned in for a kiss.

As soon as Ash's lips touched his, Brighton snapped out of his daydream, blinking as Violet looked at him. Her show was ending and he turned off the television.

"What do you want to play?" Raymond asked, flying Violet through the air to squeals of delight.

"Trucks." Violet raced to her toy box as soon as Raymond put her down, and soon the three of them were running trucks and cars across the floor. Brighton played for a while and then went to run her water. He managed to keep Ash out of his mind as he got Violet's bath ready.

She played in the tub, and Brighton ended up wet. It didn't matter—Violet's joy overshadowed his blues. Once he got her out, Brighton helped her dry off and put her in her pajamas before reading her a story. She was asleep before he finished, and Brighton kissed her good night and quietly left her little area to join Raymond in the living room, where he'd already turned out the lights.

"I'm going to go to bed." Brighton hugged Raymond and went to his room. He wasn't fit to be around other people right now, and maybe when he woke up…. Shit, he just needed some time to grieve for what could have been.

CHAPTER 9

"NO, YOU aren't going crazy, but there are times when it will be difficult for you to understand what is real and what is your head working overtime," Ash's counselor, James Marshall, said from his chair.

"But how do I understand when that is?" Ash fidgeted in his chair. This was the second appointment he'd had in the week since Brighton left, and he was as anxious as a long-tailed cat in a room full of rocking chairs, as Aunt Petey had told him once.

"This is something every combat veteran goes through to some extent or another. You need to cut yourself a little slack and not expect perfection or a quick end to these issues. You've been home a matter of weeks after years in the Army, captivity, and then debriefing." James leaned forward. "They should have had counselors for you when you were in the hospital recovering."

Ash rolled his eyes. "They did. I had a counselor who found out I was gay and decided that was the issue. She was fixated on it. So she didn't do me any good, and now here I am." He threw his arms in the air, stood, and walked to the window that looked out over a parking lot. "I know there can be enemies out there."

"Yes. It's possible. But this isn't a war zone. You're home, and it will take you some time to adjust to the fact that everyone you encounter isn't necessarily a combatant." James made some notes. "Do you want to tell me what it was that precipitated the frantic call I got a few days ago?"

Ash had known they'd get to that eventually. "A friend shared some information that the man who tortured me was allowed into this country because he had information." Ash's teeth ground together. "Then he disappeared. Please don't ask for more detail than that. But I thought and still think he could be out there and coming for me."

"Why? This is a huge country. Why put himself in danger and come for you?" James asked the question just like he did all the others, calmly. "Think about it logically. You aren't his prisoner any longer. You can fight back now, and you will if this threat turns out to be real. But what if it isn't?"

Ash sat back down. "You mean, what if this whole thing is just in my head?" He turned to scan the room, with its utilitarian gray metal furniture that had to be thirty years old. For that matter, so was the counselor.

"No. You were taught to evaluate and deal with threats, and that's what you're doing. On the battlefield, in a war zone, your conclusions might be correct. But in civilian life, the conclusions you were trained to draw might not be as helpful as they were in the field. What we need to do is help you develop new decision-making and threat-evaluation skills so you can live a more normal life. Does that sound all right to you?"

Ash nodded and took a deep breath, then released it slowly. "That sounds good." He couldn't let his reactions take over his life the way he had with Musalla. Aunt Petey had said she'd come close to smacking him at least half a dozen times.

"So I have one more question for today. What was the true cost of your overreaction?" James rested his notebook on his lap, waiting patiently, as Ash's stomach churned. For a second he thought he was going to be sick, but he kept the contents of his stomach where they were. "Usually there is something that precipitates the calls I get, especially when they're nearly frantic. Something happened, didn't it?"

"Yes. I broke a promise because I was scared and thought I had to leave to protect the ones I loved. The problem is that it cost me the one I loved most." Ash wrung his hands but, when he realized what he was doing, stilled them on his lap. "When I was held captive, in order to keep sane, I held on to Brighton, tight. I kept him in my mind, his smiling face and bright eyes, whenever I needed something to live for."

"How long had you known each other?"

"Since we were twelve." Ash smiled as he remembered the first day he met Brighton. "My mom and dad were killed, and I went to live with my aunt. She enrolled me in school, and when I walked into class that first day, Brighton was sitting in the chair next to mine. At recess he asked if I wanted to hang out with him, and after that...." Something so simple. "I came to love him in high school when we both realized we were gay, and he was there when I went away into the service." Ash told him the rest of what happened, words rushing out of him. "I can't blame him. It seems I've been leaving him behind for most of our lives... but I always came back," Ash hastily added.

"That's a very long and deep relationship. You were friends and then more," James reiterated, and Ash nodded. "So what do you think you are now?"

Ash shrugged. "I don't know."

"What do you want things to be for the two of you?"

"What I want doesn't seem to play into reality. Because it's what he wants that counts." Ash checked his watch, now anxious for this session to be over.

"Are you sure about that? What we want has a lot to do with the relationships we have and how healthy they are." James raised his eyebrows. "Tell me what you want."

"Want.... Jesus. I want to be able to sleep through the night without waking up thinking I'm back in combat. I want to have my life back. I wish I could have the life I had before I left on that last mission. Brighton and I had plans. We were going to buy a small house together, plant a garden, get a dog, maybe start a business together, something that would support us." Ash stared hard at James. "That's what I want!"

James shrugged. "And what's stopping you from having all that?" He sat back and turned to the clock next to his chair. "I'll see you next week."

To say that Ash was stunned was an understatement. He left the office and met with the receptionist to make another appointment.

"Is the same time next week all right?" she asked.

"Yes. Thank you." He smiled and took the card with his appointment information and turned to go as the phone rang. The receptionist answered it, and Ash left the small clinic in the VA office and stepped outside. It had been raining for the last two days and the pavement was still wet, but as he reached his vehicle, the clouds parted a little and the first rays of sun glinted off the hood of the truck. Ash paused, looking up at the mostly cloudy sky to catch the first patch of blue. He took a deep breath and released it, clearing his lungs.

James had been right. What was standing in the way of what Ash wanted? He wanted to say Brighton, but that wasn't true. The person standing in his way was himself. Brighton had moved into the house with him and forgiven him for what had happened between them. Brighton had been there to rub his leg and help take care of him. Ash could see it now, though he hadn't earlier. Brighton loved him.

"Holy hell…." Ash pulled open the door of the truck and got inside. He closed the door and sat behind the wheel, staring at nothing through the windshield. Ash had been the one to mess things up, and somehow he had to fix this. His mind churned with how he was going to show Brighton that he wanted the same things Brighton did.

BY THE time he reached Aunt Petey's, he was no closer to any answers. He got out of the truck and walked up to the house. He looked around carefully, as was his habit, and went inside.

"Aunt Petey?"

"I'm in here," she answered quietly, and Ash followed her voice to her room, where he found her still dressed but lying down on the bed. "I was tired." She sat up. "There was a phone call, and I wrote down the number." She handed him a scrap of paper and lay back down. "It sucks getting old."

"You're not old." Ash smiled.

"Thanks for lying to an old lady. I appreciate it." She closed her eyes. "Why are you so happy?"

"I met with the counselor, and he had some interesting things to say." He still was no closer to figuring out what he was going to do, though.

"Did he tell you that you acted like a jackass? Because if he didn't, I will. Now go on and leave me alone for an hour. I'll feel better, and then you can take me to dinner. I want a burger and some special tea."

Ash shook his head and rolled his eyes. "Fine. I'll take you to Rose's for dinner."

"And while we're at it, we'll stop by Gardner's and get you some flowers and maybe some candy. We could try jewelry, but I don't think the store is open. That's what your uncle used to bring me whenever he acted like a jackass." Aunt Petey turned and pointed to the lacquered box on the dresser. "Your uncle could be a jackass at regular intervals." She grinned and then closed her eyes. "An hour. No longer." She shooed him out, and he returned to the living room, where he put his leg up and rested it.

Ash grabbed his phone and dialed the number Aunt Petey had given him.

"Hello?"

"This is Ash…."

"Hey, it's Marty. Look…," he demurred. "They got him in Detroit." Marty paused. "I'll talk to you later." He hung up, and Ash stared at the screen, sighing and breathing freely for the first time in ten days.

"Shit." That meant he'd never been around here and that… dammit… this had been for nothing, and he'd lost Brighton anyway. He let the tension from the last week leach away and sat back, trying to return to the problem at hand. Nothing had changed, other than he had confirmation of his overreaction. Now he still had to figure out what he was going to do to show Brighton that he understood and wanted the same thing he did.

Ash had rested his leg over the past week, and it felt a lot better. He got back up and wandered out to the backyard. He turned to the huge tree in the corner that still bore the scars from his and Brighton's childhood engineering projects.

One of his aunt's old patio chairs rested against the house. Ash brushed off the old redwood seat and sat, putting his leg up on the stool that he moved from next to it. Ash pulled out his phone and filed through the contacts, his gaze stopping on one of the names.

"Ash, man, how is it going? I'm sorry I haven't been over, but things have been busy. Did you get your aunt home?" His friend Casey always talked a mile a minute. The guy had enough energy to power a small city most of the time.

"Yeah, and she loved the things we did in the house. I can't tell you how much that meant to both her and me that you all would take that time to pitch in." Ash smiled and hoped he'd managed to cover the hitch in his voice. "She's home and as happy as I've ever seen her."

"How about you? Did things work out with you and your guy?" Casey was as straight as they came, but he was also one of the most stand-up, secure men Ash had ever met. "You said you thought he had a husband and family."

"There's good news and bad news on that front. I was wrong. He's raising his sister's daughter, but the guy turned out to be his cousin. I jumped to the wrong conclusion and felt like an idiot, which seems to be a recurring theme. The idiot part, that is."

Casey chuckled a deep, throaty rumble. "What did you do?"

"Fear," Ash answered, giving voice to the ultimate enemy.

"Ah…." They all knew its touch. They'd dealt with it every day, and when it got to be too much and overwhelmed them, people died.

"I had him. He was in my life, here in the house with me, and I blew it all to hell. The thing is, I don't know how to make it better. I could try to talk to him, but that seems so lame." And so fucking full of excuses.

"Tell me about it. Justine and I are starting to work things out again. But it's hard. She keeps expecting things to be the same, and I can't do that. I'm not the same as I was. I've seen shit I can't unsee, no matter how much I wish to fucking hell I could."

"I know what you mean." It felt good to talk to someone who had been through the same kind of things he had. He and Casey had gone through basic together, and then they were assigned to the same unit for a couple of years, but they separated, and thankfully Casey and some of the other guys he knew hadn't been part of his last mission. "What did you do with Justine? You said she was keeping her distance," Ash said, hoping for some insight.

Casey sighed. "I broke down and told her. All of it. Everything." He heard Casey swallow. "I never wanted to taint her with that stuff, but in the end, I said I'd tell her the story only once and then never again, and she had to promise to forget it once it was over. I was so afraid she'd never see me the same way again. And I was right. She doesn't."

Oh crap. "What happened?"

"She understood. She said that now a lot of things made sense to her. Then she jumped at me and, well… that woman is a tiger." Casey snickered softly. "We can't expect the people in our lives to understand what's happened to us if we don't tell them."

"But all of it…?" Ash asked.

Casey hesitated. "As much of it as I've told anyone. She deserves to know who I really am." He cleared his throat. "It was hard to relive all that stuff, but in the end, she got what she needed.

Justine always knew me better than anyone else, and now she really does. There can't be secrets between us."

"I guess you're right." Even though Brighton had done his best to try to understand, Ash owed him the truth.

"We joined up to protect and serve, and that's what we did all those years. It's hard to turn it off. But Justine doesn't want someone to protect her. She wants a partner, someone to support her, and in return she's willing to do the same for me." Casey cleared his throat, and for a moment, Ash thought he might be getting emotional. Of course, that lasted only a fraction of a second, but it was enough to give Ash the idea that what he was trying to figure out wasn't unique. "That's enough of that shit." Casey cleared his throat again. "What are you going to do?"

"I haven't figured it out yet."

"You will. Hell, if I can, then you certainly will." Casey chuckled. "Just do what's in your heart." God, Ash could not believe that either of them was having this conversation. "Justine and I are trying to figure out a date for the big day."

"I can't wait," Ash told him.

"And if you get your head out of your butt, bring your Brighton. I'd like to meet him. For now, I gotta run. Talk soon."

Ash checked the time and sat in the fresh air for a little while longer before going inside to make sure Aunt Petey was up. Then he needed to get ready to take her to dinner.

ROSE HURRIED over as soon as they arrived, flustered and out of sorts. Aunt Petey seemed to understand, and when they got to the table, she placed her order for a burger and iced tea. No wink or anything. Ash ordered the meatloaf special and a Coke.

"What's going on?" he asked once Rose left.

"The fuzz," Aunt Petey explained. "She had to dump her tea, and she always gets itchy whenever that happens." She rolled her eyes.

158

"You mean, they don't know what she's doing after all these years?" Ash found it hard to believe.

"Of course they do, but she has to keep it cool. She doesn't sell it to regular customers or anything. Mostly it's us oldsters who need some help with pain and things like that. But the newbies...." Aunt Petey lightly knocked on the table. "I don't want her to get into any trouble."

"I don't either." Ash followed Rose with his eyes as she made her rounds through the restaurant, refilling glasses and taking orders. "I keep wondering what I'm going to do." He sipped from his glass. "Whenever I try to see what my life is going to look like, I see Brighton as part of the picture.... I was even seeing Violet in the picture with us."

"If that's true, then how are you going to clean up the mess you made?" Aunt Petey had a great way of cutting to the chase.

"I wish I knew. Casey told me to follow my heart."

Aunt Petey nearly choked. "He's the huge one with all the tattoos? Kinda touchy-feely for a guy like that."

"He's in love and apparently just worked things out with her. Casey has been going through a lot of the same kind of stuff I have. He gave me some advice, but I don't think Brighton will let me close enough to talk to him."

A shadow fell over their table, and Ash lifted his gaze to Raymond, Brighton's cousin, glaring at him, arms folded. "You really are a stupid piece of shit, aren't you?" He turned to Aunt Petey. "Sorry."

"Don't be. I love Ash with everything I have, but he can be an ass sometimes." She turned to him, raising her eyebrows.

"I can't believe you haven't come by at all to try to talk to him." Raymond jabbed his finger in Ash's direction. "I really thought you cared for both of them." If it were possible, fire would have shot out of his eyes. "What sort of game were you playing with him?"

"What did he tell you?" Ash asked.

159

"Everything. At least I hope he did. I debated coming over to talk to you at all. But you really seem to care for Brighton, and he needs and deserves someone to look after him. But so help me, if you're playing some game with him…."

"I'm not."

"Then let me remind you of a few things." Raymond pushed into the booth, shoving Ash over. "He watched you leave and then waited for you to return, and you didn't. I told you I picked up the pieces, and dammit, I'm doing the same thing again." Raymond got right in his face. "I'm going to give you a choice. You either figure out how you're going to make this up to him—and I'll tell you, I'm thinking diamonds or something equally amazing—or you stay away from him forever so he can move on. There's no middle ground."

"I see," Ash murmured.

"No, you don't. If you stay away, then change that little pea brain of yours in a month or so and figure you'll get him back, I'll call some friends of mine and we'll surgically remove your nuts and cook them up in an omelet for you. So you decide if he's your other half, and if he is, you go to him and tell him, beg him, give him gifts, pledge indentured servitude, whatever it takes… or you walk away and never… ever come back." Raymond stood. "I'm sorry, Aunt Petey, but it had to be said."

"I understand speaking your mind." She drank her tea and said nothing more and gave no further reaction of any kind to Ash being completely dressed down. Raymond left the table, and Aunt Petey once again looked at him as though he were the stupidest man on earth.

"Do I have to tell you what to do?" She sighed. "Sometimes you men are so dumb. Brighton loves you enough that Raymond wants you to either piss or get off the pot. So do it."

"But what if he won't let me?"

Aunt Petey leaned across the table and smacked him on the side of the head. "When have you let anything stand in the way of what you want? You don't wish-wash—you go out and get it."

Rose brought them their meals and took a seat next to Aunt Petey. "I think I'm getting too damn old for this. I love this place, I grew up here, but these legs aren't meant for me to be on them all day."

"Have you thought about selling?" Ash asked.

Rose laughed. "This place is an antique. Everything in it is old and as temperamental as I am. It still works, but it's outdated and inefficient." She sighed. "Maybe I should retire and just close up. But all I have is Social Security, and it's impossible to live on just that."

"Then find someone to buy the place and have you stay on as a manager or something. You train and help the new owners and then step back over time. This is an institution—no one wants to see it go away."

"I'll think about it," Rose said, turning to Aunt Petey. "How are you doing?"

"Good. Ash is taking care of me, and I'm able to do some things so I'm not completely useless. I've been knitting stuff for the church bazaar later this year. It keeps me busy and helps keep my hands from crippling up."

"You go ahead and eat. I'm just taking a load off for a few seconds." Rose motioned, and Ash dug into his meatloaf, which was amazing.

"How come your food tastes better than anyone else's?" Ash asked. "It tastes like home."

"My mother started this place after my dad left us. She did things by hand, and I've done it the same way she would have. There's love and care in each plate." Rose smiled and patted his hand gently. "Enjoy your dinner. I need to check on folks." She left the table, and Ash sank into his own thoughts.

He hadn't given Raymond an answer, but he wanted Brighton back more than anything else in the world. He wished he could have seen what he was doing before, but he'd thought he had everything under control. Ash didn't think he had things under control now, but at least he knew that he didn't and that he'd been overreacting. Reality for him had become different than for everyone else. He was also learning that what bothered him wasn't what drove or worried others. Ash wanted to feel safe and secure; Brighton wanted someone…. Ash damn near pounded his head. Brighton wanted the same thing. He wanted to be safe and secure, but that meant Ash needed to stay and be there for him. For Brighton, security meant not leaving.

"You know, sometimes I'm completely stupid."

"You're a man. Of course you are." Aunt Petey smiled. "Now, do you know what you're going to do?"

Ash ate faster. He did know, and he needed to get started as soon as he finished eating. An idea had formed in his mind, and he needed to see it through.

"Don't choke down your food." Aunt Petey ate her burger slowly, and when they were done, Ash paid the bill.

"Do you want me to take you home?"

"No." She stood, and he took her arm to help her outside. "Let's get you what you need so you don't mope around next week like you have this one."

"Okay." Ash helped her into the truck, then took off toward Gettysburg so he could get what he needed at the larger stores. Ash felt better knowing he had a plan. Now he just had to make it work.

CHAPTER 10

THE BELL rang downstairs, and Brighton went down to answer it. He expected to see his mother there to pick up Violet for an overnight with her grandparents. "I'm coming." He opened the door to Ash holding a huge bouquet of flowers. "What are you doing here?"

Ash stepped closer, pressing the flowers into his hands. "They caught him in Detroit."

Brighton took the flowers.

"I was stupid."

"Yeah...." Brighton wasn't buying this line again.

"I've been seeing a counselor to try to get some help. He made me see that I was out of control and didn't understand what I was doing to the people around me. I didn't realize what it was you needed, even though you told me. I still didn't see it. All I could understand was what was in my own head. But I think I understand what you need, and I messed it up."

"I accept your apology, but...." Brighton's heart leaped that Ash was here in front of him. He looked like he hadn't slept in about the same amount of time since Brighton had gotten a decent night's rest.

"I know. I've messed so many things up since I got back. I should have come to see you and not jumped to conclusions, and I should have known that running away wasn't the answer. You were there for me and tried to help me, but I was too deep into my own head to understand that. I kept thinking that as long as I came back, everything would be all right. But it wasn't, because it was the leaving that tore you apart." Ash held out his hand.

Brighton stared at it, trying to decide what he was going to do. He wanted to take it, to bridge the gap between them, but he hesitated.

"I want to show you something if you can come with me," Ash said quietly.

"Let me go put these in water." No one had ever given him flowers before, and Brighton turned, smelling them as he smiled. He went upstairs, and Ash followed. "How's your leg?"

"Better. I've been staying off it and letting it heal. Like I should have been all along." Ash seemed much calmer now. Those last few days had been frantic, with Ash checking the perimeter and worrying about intruders and Musalla. "I called the VA after you left, and I've seen my counselor twice."

Brighton nodded and got a vase from under the sink, filled it with water, and slid the flowers into it. "You weren't before?" It was the one thing Brighton hadn't thought to ask.

"No. I thought I understood things and could handle it on my own. I was so wrong. James is a nice man, and maybe you'd be willing to go with me sometime. It would help if he heard about how I am from other people."

"I can do that." Brighton sighed, grabbing the counter. "Ash, I…." His voice faltered.

"I know." Ash came closer. "I missed you, Brighton. I realize I messed up, but I missed you as soon as you walked out the door. I just didn't know what to do or say to get you to come back. And I don't know if what I have to say and what I want you to see is good enough, but I want to try."

Brighton didn't turn around, but he felt the heat radiating off Ash's body as he got even closer. Brighton tightened his grip on the edge of the counter, hoping Ash took him in his arms and dreading the touch at the same time, because if Ash took him, wrapping him in his strong arms, there was no way Brighton could say no to him, and he needed to say no. He needed some separation in order to keep his head clear. Brighton couldn't go through what he already had any longer.

"Where's Violet?" Ash asked just as she came racing out of her room toward Ash with a grin on her face.

"I missed you, Mr. Ash," she cried, and Ash turned away from him, giving Brighton some breathing room. Ash hugged Violet, who dropped her backpack on the floor. "I missed you a lot."

"I missed you too," Ash told her, caressing her hair and holding her.

"Your grandma is going to be here in just a few minutes," Brighton told her gently. "Go on and watch for her." Brighton picked up the backpack and set it on the nearby chair as she raced to the front window.

"She's here!" Violet raced back, and Brighton got her pack on and walked Violet down the stairs.

He said goodbye to her and gave his mother a hug, then watched Violet wave as his mother pulled away. Brighton stood out on the sidewalk and turned around, glancing upward. Ash was inside, and Brighton needed to make a decision on how he was going to handle this.

Opening the door, he decided to tell Ash to go home. He'd already said his piece before, and he wasn't going to go through all this leaving shit anymore. He'd find someone who was happy being with him and who didn't fucking run all the time. Brighton's heart couldn't take the bruises anymore.

Ash met him at the door at the top of the stairs, and all the words that had been on the tip of Brighton's tongue sprouted wings and flew away. "I've been just as miserable as it's possible to be." Ash hugged him as soon as Brighton closed the door. "Do you remember, before I left, you and I made some plans?"

Brighton nodded, hugging Ash in return. "Yeah, I remember."

"Come on. I have some things I want to show you." Ash didn't release him, and they stood there for a while, just soaking it in.

Brighton tightened his hug. He wanted to believe that this could be real and that what Ash had said was true, he really did. But he couldn't allow himself to be caught up in things again. It hurt too damn much when it ended.

"Ash... I have to...."

Ash squeezed him tight, cradling his head with one hand. "I know how you feel. I've spent a lot of time trying to put myself in your shoes these last few days once I got my head pulled out of my butt. I think I understand how I hurt you, and I don't ever want to do that again. So will you come with me?" Ash asked, his voice as soft as a spring rain.

"Okay." Brighton let go and went to get his keys. His heart pounded, but he didn't dare let himself get too far ahead. He grabbed them off the counter and followed Ash out of the apartment and down to his truck, locking the doors as he went. Except they didn't get in the truck. Ash took his hand, entwining their fingers, and led him down the street. "Are you sure you should be walking this far?"

"My leg is getting better, and the therapist said I could walk as long as I was careful and the ground was level. Besides, we aren't going far." He seemed so pleased as they walked toward the Apple Diner.

"Are you hungry?" Brighton asked as they stopped outside the windows.

"No. See, I went to dinner with Aunt Petey here a few days ago and was talking to Rose. She's getting up there in years and is looking to spend her days doing something other than running her feet off."

"She wants to sell?" Brighton moved closer.

"Yes, she does. Rose owns the building and the restaurant. She lives upstairs, but I was thinking that we could live at Aunt Petey's. I can't leave her alone, but there would be room for Violet. We could also get a dog for her, put in a garden—all the things we said we wanted. There are a bunch of things we'd need to work out, but you and I could have it all."

"Who does the cooking?" Brighton looked up the front of the building to the sign, trying to see it as theirs.

"Frankie. He's been working here for eight years and seems happy. As long as we treat him right, he'll stay. Eventually I'll work in the kitchen, and you could do what Rose does if you want, wait tables and see to the customers. You'd be great at that. We'll fix the floors, paint the walls, and I'm thinking new tables and repair the booths. Keep it looking old-fashioned, but make it our own too."

"But it's a lot of work." Though Brighton wasn't afraid of that. At least they'd be working for themselves.

"We'd be open for lunch and dinner and closed on Sundays." He turned to Brighton, who felt the heat from Ash's eyes. "It would be ours, yours and mine. We'd learn Rose's recipes and then maybe develop some of our own." Ash had almost as much excitement in his eyes as he had when they were in bed together—almost.

"Are you sure about something like this?" Brighton was a little overwhelmed.

"I worked in the drive-in outside of town, the one that's closed now, when I was in high school, remember? I did a lot of different things there. And you waited tables in Gettysburg that summer." Ash took his hand. "If this isn't what you want, then tell me. We can do something else. I have to find some work, regardless."

"I know. But I never pictured myself running a restaurant." Suddenly the picture in Brighton's mind shifted. For the last little while, it had been him and Violet. Now Ash was back, and he could see Violet sitting in "her" booth doing her homework or coloring, Ash and him in the seat across from her. This was the kind of thing he wanted, what he'd always dreamed of. "But I think we can do anything we put our minds to."

"Are you sure?" Ash asked.

Brighton scoffed. "I'm not sure of much right now."

"We can think about it if you want. Rose isn't going anywhere." Ash led him away from the restaurant and to the truck. Ash seemed really excited, practically bouncing as he drove out of town to Aunt Petey's house. Instead of going inside, Ash walked him around the side of the house to the backyard.

"What's this?"

"A spot for your garden. My friend Casey had a tiller and turned this spot. Uncle Matt used to have a garden here, and I thought you'd like it." Ash grinned. "Do you remember sneaking tomatoes out of the garden?"

Brighton did. "And the cucumbers." He moved closer to Ash without really thinking about it.

"There's one more thing." Ash hurried over to the back door, limping a little, but that didn't seem to stop him for a second. He went inside and came right out, carrying something in his arms. As Ash got closer, he saw the pink nose of a puppy. "We always talked about getting a dog."

Brighton saw the size of the pup as he got closer. "He's...."

Ash handed over the large puppy, who lifted his nose to lick the underside of Brighton's chin. "Do you remember when we went to that street festival in Carlisle and that guy had a Great Dane? He just sat there while all the kids petted him. He was gorgeous, and you said you wanted a dog like that...." Ash raised his eyebrows and turned his gaze to the puppy.

"No way! How did you find one?" Brighton cradled the puppy a little closer. "He's going to be huge."

"But we have room, and look at him." Ash stood next to Brighton, and the puppy stuck out his nose to catch Ash's cheek with his tongue. "Aunt Petey likes him, but he's for you."

Brighton blinked. "I think I get it now. We always said we wanted a home with a garden and a puppy and a business of our own. That was the plan."

"Yeah. Better late than never."

Brighton understood. Ash wasn't telling him how important Brighton was—he was trying to show him by making their wishes and dreams come true. "I can't believe you remembered." He had honestly thought that, after all that had happened, Ash had forgotten or given up on their dreams, but he shared them. "I thought they were gone. That you had changed enough that you didn't want the same things anymore."

"Some things might change, but I always wanted you. You were with me for the worst parts of my life, getting me through it, and you've been there for the best parts of my life so far. Now, I hope you'll go with me as we make a life together. Every time I look at my future, you're part of it... and so is Violet." Ash stroked the puppy's head as he leaned in closer. "You and Violet are my future."

Brighton swallowed hard. "So no more leaving?"

"Not unless the two of you come with me." Ash sighed. "This is my home, you're my home, and I'm not going to leave it. I always had a place I needed to go, either because of the Army or because I couldn't sit still. But I know now that every time I left, I was leaving you behind. I went off, and you stayed here, waiting for me to come home. I just expected that you'd be here when I came home, and then that last time, a year ago, I thought you hadn't been, that you'd moved on."

"But—" Brighton began, but Ash silenced him with a touch.

"You had every right to move on, and when you didn't and you wanted me, all I did was try to leave again. You deserve better than that. You deserve someone who will stay here with you and build the life we planned together." Ash blinked. "I just hope that person is me."

Brighton set the puppy on the grass, and he took a few steps before bounding toward a cricket, all gangly legs and wagging tail. "You were always that person." Brighton wiped his eyes. "I dreamed with you, loved with you... all I needed was for you to come back. Really come back to me. And you finally did." Brighton hugged Ash and brought their lips together. "But if you try to leave again...."

Ash chuckled, holding him. "Raymond was pretty graphic."

"You talked to him?" Brighton asked in surprise.

"I saw him a few days ago at the Apple Diner. Let's just say he did the talking. You know, your cousin is a terrorist." Ash grinned.

"That guy can make better threats than North Korea. He was pretty clear in how he felt."

"I'm sorry." Brighton wondered what Raymond had actually told Ash.

"Don't be. I should send him a fruit basket or something. He made me see that if I wanted you in my life, I needed to pull my head out of my butt and make a damned decision, then go for what I wanted." Ash hugged him tighter. "You are the person I always wanted, Brighton. You're my other half, and I've loved you for years. And I'll never stop loving you, no matter what." Ash kissed him again, enfolding Brighton in his arms, using his strength to hold him.

Ash's love poured into him with such ferocious determination that Brighton couldn't stop it. His entire body heated, sweat broke out on his arms, and he held on, never wanting this to end. The kiss brought him back, and Brighton knew there was no doubt that if Ash weren't in his life, he'd be looking over his shoulder to find out where he was.

"I love you too. And I waited so long to have you back."

"You're not going to have to wait anymore. I'm right here, and I promise I'm not going anywhere." Ash kissed him again as the puppy ran circles around their legs.

"What are we going to call him?" Brighton asked, then raced across the yard as the puppy headed for the woods. He caught him, lifted him off his legs, and carried him back to where Ash waited, smiling as widely as Brighton had ever seen.

"I was thinking you could name him," Ash answered as he got close enough for the puppy to lick him.

"You know, Violet is going to come unglued when she sees him," Brighton observed as he ran potential names through his head. He wasn't coming up with anything interesting.

"I know. I can see the two of them playing out here, getting into as much trouble as you and I used to." Ash put an arm around

170

Brighton's waist as they looked over the familiar back lawn. "This backyard saw so much of us growing up together."

"Yeah, and if that tree right over there could talk, its leaves would turn red from embarrassment, and then it would tell all our secrets. I can see the scars from our treehouse."

"I tore it down. It was going to fall, and I didn't want to leave a mess for Aunt Petey."

"I know. We built it a long time ago. We were kids, and it's surprising it stayed up as long as it did and that your aunt and uncle allowed it." They'd loved both of them. Aunt Petey and Uncle Matt had been there for both of them without question. Brighton always had a safe place because of their generosity.

The puppy began to squirm, so Brighton set him down once again. He made for some bushes and squatted down.

"You're a real good boy," Ash said as he stroked the pup's head after he did his business. "I already had to clean up a mess in the house. Once. I'm hoping he'll be really easy to train."

"I suspect so. He's really smart." Brighton leaned down, and the puppy bounded over. "I think I'm going to call you Dante." Brighton rubbed his head, and the pup licked his fingers. "Do you like that, Dante?" Brighton petted him, and the pup's tail wagged his entire backside.

"Why Dante?" Ash asked.

"It popped into my head. I was thinking of all you've been through and what we've been through together. We sort of went into hell and came out the other side, so I think Dante is appropriate." Brighton scooped up the puppy, and Ash opened the back door. Brighton went inside and set the puppy on the floor. He raced through the house.

"Hey!" Aunt Petey said. "You have your own toys." By the time Brighton got to the living room, Dante was sitting on the floor in front of her chair as Aunt Petey gathered up her yarn. "These aren't toys and will give you indigestion." She picked up a ball and rolled it along the floor. Dante skittered after it with all the energy puppies have.

"I like him as long as he learns to leave my yarn alone." She glared after Dante, who brought back the ball so Aunt Petey could throw it again. He obviously caught on quickly. She rolled the ball away, and he bounded after it.

Ash took Brighton's arm. "I have one more thing to show you," he said, guiding him toward the stairs.

Dante climbed up behind them and wandered down the hall, sniffing all the doors, his tail wagging like crazy. He was dark blond and was going to be incredibly stunning once he grew up.

Ash opened the door to the room next to his and held it so Brighton could go inside. "I made up this room for Violet." He grinned. "The bed was here and the wallpaper has violets on it, and I thought she'd like it. I found the dollhouse in the attic and asked Aunt Petey about it. Uncle Matt made it, convinced he and Aunt Petey were going to fill this house with children. When they didn't, he put it in the attic, and it's been there ever since. Aunt Petey said she was delighted that Violet would get to use it."

Brighton took a step inside, his eyes wide. "What about the rest?"

"I picked out the rug and bedspread in pink for her. I thought she'd really like it. And I left the pale lace curtains, but we can get whatever Violet would like."

Brighton looked around, taking in the entire room. "Why does the closet door have a big black square thing hanging on it?"

"Chalkboard paint," Ash told him and Brighton gasped. That was brilliant.

"This is so perfect for her. What's that box in the corner?" It was made out of wood and beautifully finished.

"I found that in the attic too. It's one of Uncle Matt's toolboxes. He made it himself and finished it. Aunt Petey said he treated his tools like they were gold. I took the trays out, but the box is sanded smooth on the inside, so I thought Violet could use it as a toy box. It's also sturdy enough for her to sit or even stand on it." Ash caught his gaze, and Brighton wiped his eyes on his sleeve.

"You thought of everything." Brighton watched as Dante jumped on the bed, making himself at home. "Come off there." Brighton lifted him, and Ash followed him out of the door before opening the door to his room.

"I brought in a second dresser for you, and there is room in the closet. I want both of you to feel like this is your home. There is another room right down the hall that was Aunt Petey's. I think we should leave it as it is for now. If she's ever able to move back upstairs, then I want her room available for her."

"Of course." Brighton leaned closer and Ash kissed him. "This is so sweet and thoughtful of you." He blinked as Ash stood upright once again.

"You're all important to me… you're family… my family." Ash stroked Dante's head. "All of you. And I love you."

Brighton couldn't have asked for a better declaration. "I love you too, first, last, and always." He set the puppy down on the floor and took Ash in his arms. "I first let you in my heart when you kissed me in the treehouse. I loved you when you came and went because of your time in the service, and I held you in my heart when I thought you were dead." Brighton swallowed hard. "I could never figure out how to replace you with anyone else."

"I was the same. When I thought you had found someone else, it took me a year to be able to come back here. I…." Ash's voice faltered. "Even through all that… I still held you with me."

Brighton held Ash tighter. "I'll never let you go."

"Neither will I." Ash leaned in again, and Brighton lifted his head upward, their lips meeting.

EPILOGUE

BRIGHTON SNUGGLED deeper under the covers to keep the cold air outside his warm cocoon at bay.

"Uncle Brighton!" Violet patted his head, and he wanted to growl. There was no way it was morning already. And even if it was, he was tired as all hell. "It's time to get up." The bouncing started then, and seconds later her weight landed on top of him as she jumped on the bed. "It's Christmas, and Santa came last night! I heard reindeer bells!"

"I did too." Brighton rolled over, tickling her before tucking Violet under the covers. Ash groaned behind him, and Brighton blinked and looked at the clock. Another weight settled on the bed, this one shaking it as a hundred twenty pounds of Great Dane settled across the end. "It's five in the morning, and while Santa might have come, you need to go back to bed."

"I wanna stay here," she whined slightly.

"Dante, get on the floor," Ash said in that Army voice of his, and a telltale shaking of the mattress and a thump followed. Brighton lifted his head just enough to see Dante settle on his dog bed in the corner, lying down and looking longingly back at Brighton.

"Santa likes it when girls are good and sleep in their own beds," Brighton said gently, and Violet climbed out from under the covers. He did the same and went to tuck her back into her own bed before rejoining Ash in theirs. Neither of them was above using Santa to get her to do what they wanted. After all, that power would end in a few hours... until next year.

"She thinks there's a ghost in the house," Ash said softly, "and she's afraid of her."

"I told you not to let her stay up and watch that haunted mansion movie." Brighton closed his eyes and wondered how long it would be before Dante figured it was safe to try getting on the bed again. That dog would sleep under the covers with them if he thought he could get away with it. Brighton got up one more time to put one of Dante's blankets over him, and he settled down with a sigh. Brighton went back to bed, Ash pulled him closer, and sleep caught up to him quickly.

The next time Violet came in, it was after seven, and Brighton reluctantly pushed back the covers. "Okay. You go put on your robe and see if Aunt Petey is up, but don't go downstairs." Having them all in the house appeared to have worked wonders. Aunt Petey had asked to be moved back upstairs to her room three months ago, and she seemed to be turning back the clock.

"I heard her," Violet said.

"Then go see if she's ready to go downstairs while Ash and I get dressed." Brighton blinked and forced his body to get moving. He and Ash had taken over the diner at the end of the summer, and Brighton had never worked so hard in his life. He loved every second of it, but today was an extra day off, and he wished he could sleep in a little bit longer.

"Come on, honey. It's Christmas, and Santa might have brought something really special." Ash popped him on the butt and then got out of bed. Sometimes Ash was a bigger kid than Violet. Ash dressed and called Dante, who trotted out of the room after him. Brighton heard their steps outside the door as he dressed, and by the time Violet and Aunt Petey were ready, he led them down the stairs.

All the lights had been turned on, and the living room twinkled with thousands of sparkles. Violet raced to the tree, jumped up and down, and then fell to the floor to play with the unwrapped gifts Santa had brought for her.

"I'm going to make some coffee," Aunt Petey said, walking toward the kitchen.

175

"Thanks." Brighton took a seat on the sofa, with Ash next to him.

"I called Raymond, and he's on his way over with Ethan." Ash grinned. Those two had been seeing each other whenever possible for months now, and Brighton was hoping one of them would figure out what they wanted to do. Still, Ethan coming to Raymond's for the holidays was a big step.

"When can we open the rest of the presents?" Violet asked.

"After Uncle Raymond gets here, we'll do stockings, and then after breakfast, we'll open presents." Brighton yawned and sat back, ready to fall asleep. Dante rested his head on his lap, and Brighton leaned on Ash, closing his eyes.

Of course he didn't get to go back to sleep. Raymond and Ethan arrived, and stockings were passed out and goodies dug for.

Brighton pulled a small box out of the bottom of his and turned to Ash. "What's this?"

Ash took the box and slid off the sofa onto his knees. Brighton heard Aunt Petey gasp and saw her hold Violet in front of her.

"Brighton." Ash opened the box, showing him the ring inside. "I love you, and I want to make the family we have permanent. So, Brighton, will you marry me?" Ash pulled out the ring, and Brighton nodded, unable to find his voice.

"Yes," he finally managed to gasp. "Yes." He smiled as Ash slipped the gold band with a line of small diamonds onto his finger.

"Merry Christmas," Ash whispered and kissed him.

For a few moments, the others faded to the background. Brighton wound his arms around Ash's neck, briefly deepening the kiss, and then pulled back.

"I love you… for always."

Brighton nodded. "Always." Then he kissed him again.

ANDREW GREY grew up in western Michigan with a father who loved to tell stories and a mother who loved to read them. Since then he has lived all over the country and traveled throughout the world. He has a master's degree from the University of Wisconsin-Milwaukee and now works full-time on his writing. Andrew's hobbies include collecting antiques, gardening, and leaving his dirty dishes anywhere but in the sink (particularly when writing). He considers himself blessed with an accepting family, fantastic friends, and the world's most supportive and loving husband. Andrew currently lives in beautiful historic Carlisle, Pennsylvania.

Email: andrewgrey@comcast.net
Website: www.andrewgreybooks.com

CAN'T LIVE
WITHOUT YOU

ANDREW
GREY

Forever Yours: Book One

Justin Hawthorne worked hard to realize his silver-screen dreams, making his way from small-town Pennsylvania to Hollywood and success. But it hasn't come without sacrifice. When Justin's father kicked him out for being gay, George Miller's family offered to take him in, but circumstances prevented it. Now Justin is back in town and has come face to face with George, the man he left without so much as a good-bye… and the man he's never stopped loving.

Justin's disappearance hit George hard, but he's made a life for himself as a home nurse and finds fulfillment in helping others. When he sees Justin again, George realizes the hole in his heart never mended, and he isn't the only one in need of healing. Justin needs time out of the public eye to find himself again, and George and his mother cannot turn him away. As they stay together in George's home, old feelings are rekindled. Is a second chance possible when everything George cares about is in Pennsylvania and Justin must return to his career in California? First they'll have to deal with the reason for Justin's abrupt departure all those years ago.

www.dreamspinnerpress.com

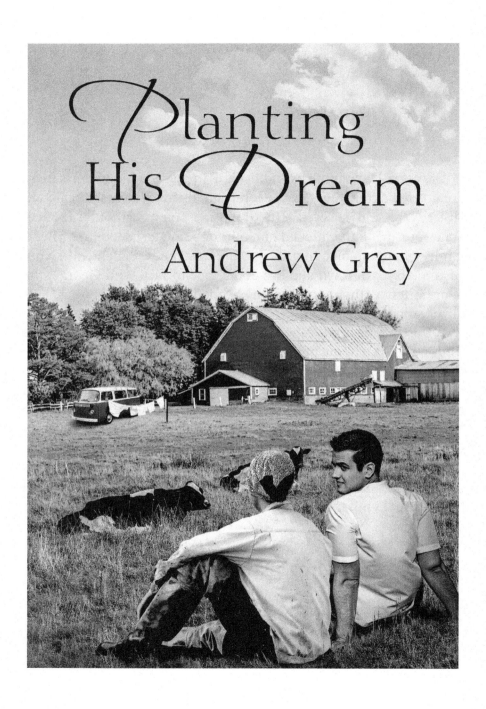

Planting His Dream

Andrew Grey

Planting Dreams: Book One

Foster dreams of getting away, but after his father's death, he has to take over the family dairy farm. It soon becomes clear his father hasn't been doing the best job of running it, so not only does Foster need to take over the day-to-day operations, he also needs to find new ways of bringing in revenue.

Javi has no time to dream. He and his family are migrant workers, and daily survival is a struggle, so they travel to anywhere they can get work. When they arrive in their old van, Foster arranges for Javi to help him on the farm.

To Javi's surprise, Foster listens to his ideas and actually puts them into action. Over days that turn into weeks, they grow to like and then care for each other, but they come from two very different worlds, and they both have responsibilities to their families that neither can walk away from. Is it possible for them to discover a dream they can share? Perhaps they can plant their own and nurture it together to see it grow, if their different backgrounds don't separate them forever.

www.dreamspinnerpress.com

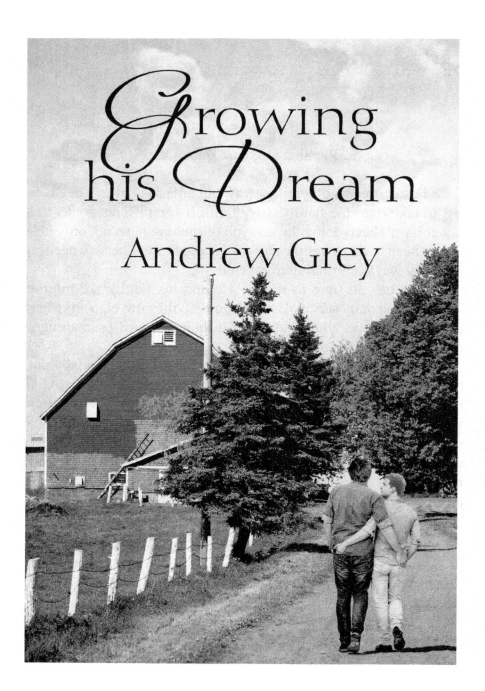

Sequel to *Planting His Dream*
Planting Dreams: Book Two

Love can grow in even the harshest conditions.

Life has been a struggle for Lachlan Buttar ever since his
mother passed away and left him unprepared to take care of
himself. He's gone from homeless to staying with a local minister,
but it soon becomes clear he will be better off, and safer, on his
own. Fortunately Foster and Javi agree to take Lachlan in and offer
him a real home on their dairy farm.

It's there that Lachlan meets another of the workers, local
farmer Abe Armitage. Though the attraction between them is
instant, Abe refuses to act on it until Lachlan returns his interest.
By then, strong feelings have taken root, and a passionate romance
quickly blossoms. But both men carry baggage that could crush any
chance of happiness together, particularly since Lachlan witnessed
a crime, and there are those who will do anything to make sure he
cannot reveal what he's seen.

www.dreamspinnerpress.com

SETTING
the HOOK
ANDREW GREY

Love's Charter: Book One

It could be the catch of a lifetime.

William Westmoreland escapes his unfulfilling Rhode Island existence by traveling to Florida twice a year and chartering Mike Jansen's fishing boat to take him out on the Gulf. The crystal-blue water and tropical scenery isn't the only view William enjoys, but he's never made his move. A vacation romance just isn't on his horizon.

Mike started his Apalachicola charter fishing service as a way to care for his daughter and mother, putting their safety and security ahead of the needs of his own heart. Denying his attraction becomes harder with each of William's visits.

William and Mike's latest fishing excursion starts with a beautiful day, but a hurricane's erratic course changes everything, stranding William. As the wind and rain rage outside, the passion the two men have been trying to resist for years crashes over them. In the storm's wake, it leaves both men yearning to prolong what they have found. But real life pulls William back to his obligations. Can they find a way to reduce the distance between them and discover a place where their souls can meet? The journey will require rough sailing, but the bright future at the end might be worth the choppy seas.

www.dreamspinnerpress.com

EBB and FLOW

ANDREW GREY

Sequel to *Setting the Hook*
Love's Charter: Book Two

To achieve happiness, they'll have to find the courage to be their own men.

As first mate on a charter fishing boat, Billy Ray meets a lot of people, but not one of them has made him as uncomfortable as Skippy—because he's drawn to Skippy as surely as the moon pulls the tides, and he's almost as powerless to resist. Billy Ray has spent his life denying who he is to avoid the wrath of his religious father, and he can't allow anyone to see through his carefully built façade.

Skippy is only in town on business and will have to return to Boston once he's through. After all, his father has certain expectations, and him staying in Florida is not one of them. But he doesn't count on Billy Ray capturing his attention and touching his heart.

Billy Ray doesn't realize just how much he and Skippy have in common, though. They're both living to please their fathers instead of following their own dreams—a fact that becomes painfully obvious when they get to know each other and realize how much joy they've denied themselves. While they can't change the past, they can begin a future together and make up for lost time—as long as they're willing to face the consequences of charting their own course.

www.dreamspinnerpress.com

ANDREW
GREY

LEGAL
ARTISTRY

An Art Series novel

Years ago, Dieter Krumpf's grandmother died and left him
everything, including a photo album containing pictures of the art
collection she left behind when her family fled the Nazis. Now,
Dieter is calling on the services of a lawyer, Gerald Young, to
determine whether his family's legacy might be returned to him.

Gerald doesn't hold out much hope that the paintings will
be returned, but Dieter's earnestness speaks to him and he agrees
to help. At first he concludes that while Dieter has a case, suing
in Austria isn't practical. But Gerald is a good lawyer, and as his
feelings for Dieter develop, so does his determination to win the
case. Together, Gerald and Dieter navigate research, hearings, and
a dysfunctional family in the pursuit of fine art—and discover the
art of love along the way.

www.dreamspinnerpress.com

CPSIA information can be obtained
at www.ICGtesting.com
Printed in the USA
BVOW06s2346310817
493634BV00012B/245/P

9 781635 339505